# The Story House

To Sidney James, with love *VF*

For my dad ('coz he's brill!) *SY*

First published in 2004
by Orion Children's Books
a division of the Orion Publishing Group Ltd
Orion House
5 Upper St Martin's Lane
London WC2H 9EA

Text copyright © Vivian French 2004
Illustrations copyright © Selina Young 2004
Designed by Sarah Hodder

The right of Vivian French and Selina Young to be identified as the author
and illustrator respectively of this work has been asserted.

A catalogue record for this book is available from the British Library

Printed in Thailand

# The Story House

Time to go inside and meet everyone.

Vivian French

illustrated by

Selina Young

Let's see what's on the next page.

Orion
Children's Books

# CONTENTS

I can't wait to start reading

# THE STORY HOUSE

*Far away from here – but not too far away – there's a house, a very special house. It has a chimney, a front door, a back door, a great many windows, a great many rooms and a weathercock on the roof. Outside is a garden … a garden full of flowers.*

*What's inside the house? Children and dogs and cats and guinea pigs, rabbits and mice and spiders – and a ghost.*

*Is he scary?*

*Not at all. He's a tired old ghost and he spends most of his time dozing.*

*Just now he's asleep in a basket by the big front door, even though it's nearly night time.*

*Look! Someone is slithering quietly through the keyhole.*

*Someone is creeping closer.*

*Someone is shaking the old ghost's arm and a little voice says, "Big Ghost! Big Ghost! TELL ME A STORY!"*

*Big Ghost opens his eyes and yawns. "What's that?"*

*"It's me! It's Little Ghost! I've come to visit! Mama Ghost has gone haunting and I'm bored bored bored! PLEASE will you tell me a story?"*

*Big Ghost stretches a huge stretch. "What story would you like, Little Ghost?"*

*Little Ghost climbs happily on to Big Ghost's knee. He looks round and sees the big old cat asleep on the mat.*

*"Tell me a story about that cat," he says.*

*Big Ghost nods. "That's Fat Freda," he says. "I'll tell you a story about some kittens."*

# WEEK 1

## The Four Little Kittens

Once upon a time there were four little kittens. Their names were Kitty Puss, Kitty Pretty, Kitty Purr and Tom and one fine day their mother promised to take them out. They were going to visit Aunt Tulip, a very beautiful cat, so Fat Freda sent the kittens downstairs to wait while she combed her whiskers and put on her bow and bell.

"I won't be long, my dears," she said. "Make sure you are all clean and tidy. I can't take dirty little kittens to see Aunt Tulip." And she settled down in front of her mirror.

Kitty Puss sat in the hallway and washed her ears. Kitty Pretty sat in the hallway washing her paws. Kitty Purr sat in the hallway washing her face. Their brother Tom was in the hallway too, but he was chasing a beetle.

"Meeow," said Kitty Puss. "Are your ears clean, Tom?"

"No," said Tom, and he pounced. The beetle scuttled under a cupboard.

"Meeow," said Kitty Pretty. "Are your paws clean, Tom?"

Oops! I hope Tom hasn't seen me.

8

"No," said Tom and he bounced up and down. The beetle stayed where it was.

"Meeow," said Kitty Purr. "Is your face clean, Tom?"

"No," said Tom and he rolled on to his tummy and patted at the cupboard with his paws. The beetle shut its eyes and went to sleep.

"Mother will be cross," said Kitty Puss.

"Very cross," said Kitty Pretty.

"Very cross INDEED," said Kitty Purr.

Tom took no notice. He thought he could see another beetle in the corner.

"Mother told us to be clean and tidy," said Kitty Puss. "She said if we weren't clean and tidy then she wouldn't take us out."

"*We're* clean and tidy," boasted Kitty Pretty. "She'll take *us.*"

"*You'll* have to stay here," said Kitty Purr. "And you won't get to go and visit Aunt Tulip!"

"I don't like visiting Aunt Tulip," said Tom. "She always tells me to be good and to sit still and she won't let me run and jump and bounce."

"But today Aunt Tulip's going to take us fishing," said Kitty Pretty.

"FISHING?" said Tom.

"Down by the stream," said Kitty Purr.

"The STREAM?" said Tom.

"We're going to catch little fishes for our tea!" said Kitty Puss and she licked her lips. "YUM YUM!"

Tom sat very still. He looked at his clean and tidy little sisters and he looked at his own four muddy paws. He scratched his ears and he thought very hard. Very hard indeed. Then he sighed loudly.

"What's the matter?" asked Kitty Puss.

"He wants to come with us," said Kitty Purr.

"Oh no I don't," said Tom. "I was just thinking how sad I'll be when you come home again without your tails."

All three kittens jumped up.

"What do you mean?" asked Kitty Pretty. "Why won't we have our tails?"

Tom opened his eyes wide. "The little fishes will eat them, of course!" he said.

Kitty Purr, Kitty Pretty and Kitty Puss stared at him.

"No they won't!" said Kitty Purr.

"Will they really?" asked Kitty Puss.

"HOW will they?" asked Kitty Pretty.

Tom laughed his very best pretend laugh. "Meeow! But that's how you catch little fishes! Didn't mother tell you? You sit on the edge of the stream and you let your tails hang down in the water. Then, when a little fishy bites the end of your tail, FLIP! You toss it on to the bank!"

Kitty Purr looked anxious.

Kitty Pretty's fur stood on end.

Kitty Puss began to cry.

Tom waved a paw in the air. "Of course," he said, "there is *another* way of catching little fishes. But you have to know how."

Tom's three little sisters rushed towards him.

"Tell us, Tom!" they begged.

"Please!" said Kitty Puss.

"Pretty please!" said Kitty Pretty.

"Pretty pretty please with a cherry on the top!" said Kitty Purr.

Tom pulled at a whisker. "OK," he said. "Watch me – and do EXACTLY what I do."

His three little sisters nodded eagerly.

"First of all you run outside and paddle your paws in the mud, so the fishes can't hear you coming."

Three little kittens skipped outside and paddled their paws in the mud.

"Then you rub mud on your nose so the little fishes can't see you."

Three little kittens carefully rubbed mud on their pink noses.

"Then you roll in the dust, just for luck."

Three little kittens rolled in the dust.

"MERRRRROWWWW!" said a terrible voice. "WHATEVER ARE YOU DOING?"

Look at all those muddy paws.

Their mother leapt down the stairs. She was dressed in her very best bow and bell and she looked very cross INDEED.

Kitty Puss, Kitty Pretty and Kitty Purr stopped rolling.

Tom stopped cleaning his face. He had already given his paws and ears a quick lick and a polish.

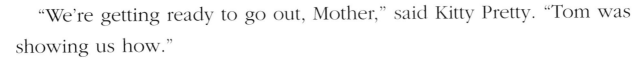

"We're getting ready to go out, Mother," said Kitty Pretty. "Tom was showing us how."

Mother Cat glared at her dirty daughters.

"MEEOW!" she said. "What NAUGHTY little kittens you are. How can I take you to see Aunt Tulip looking like that? Tom! You are a good, clean, tidy kitten – and YOU shall come with me – all on your own!"

Tom smiled an ENORMOUS smile and skipped up to his mother's side.

"But we were only getting ready to catch the little fishes," wailed Kitty Puss.

"What little fishes?" Mother Cat stared at Kitty Purr.

"You said we were going fishing with Aunt Tulip," sniffed Kitty Pretty.

"FISHING?" said Mother Cat. "I said we were going to help Aunt Tulip with her WASHING!"

Kitty Purr, Kitty Puss and Kitty Pretty watched Tom trail miserably down the garden path after Mother Cat. He was carrying a basket of clothes pegs.

"Do you *really* need muddy paws to catch little fishes?" asked Kitty Purr.

"I don't know," said Kitty Pretty. "But we could try catching beetles. I've just seen one scuttle out from under the cupboard …"

*Little Ghost sighs happily. "That's a good story," he says. "Now tell me another story about this house."*

*Big Ghost shakes his head. "Not just now, Little Ghost," he says. "I can hear your mama calling you."*

*"I don't think she'd mind waiting," Little Ghost says hopefully.*

*Big Ghost picks Little Ghost up and carries him to the front door. "I think she might," he says. "Why don't you come back here next week and I'll tell you a story about the people who live here?"*

*Little Ghost turns quite blue with excitement. "Oh, YES! And can I come EVERY week?"*

*Big Ghost smiles. "If your mama says you can, Little Ghost. This house is full of stories. Now hurry through that keyhole! I'll see you next week!"*

# WEEK 2

It's a week now since Little Ghost came visiting. It's late in the
evening and Big Ghost is snoring on top of the kitchen cupboard.

Little Ghost comes tiptoeing through the wide open kitchen door.
"BOO!"

Big Ghost jumps so high that his head goes through the ceiling.

"It's me!" shouts Little Ghost. "I'm back and I've come for my story!"

Big Ghost settles himself in the vegetable rack among the cabbages.
"So I see," he says.

Little Ghost squeezes in beside him. "Tell me about the people who live here."

"All right," says Big Ghost and he laughs. "I'll tell you a story about a funny smell."

## The Funny Smell

Once upon a time there was a big house and a great
many people lived inside. There were the twins, Tia and
Tim, their big brother Ross and their little brother Jason.
Their mum lived there too, but their dad lived down the
road. He came to visit a lot, so Tia called him Visiting Dad.

As well as Ross and Tia and Tim and Jason there was Daisy B. Mum was her mum, but her dad was Julius and he lived in the house too. Everyone called him Julius – even Daisy B. It made things much less muddly. Last, but not least, there was Granny Annie, but sometimes Tim and Tia saw a floaty kind of person wandering up and down the stairs. Tia said it was a ghost, but Mum said she'd never seen it and she thought Tia and Tim were imagining things.

> *"Is that you?" breathed Little Ghost. "Big Ghost, is that you?"*
>
> *"Yes," said Big Ghost. "But don't interrupt."*

There were lots of animals in the house. Tiny and Hunter were the dogs; Tiny was a very little dog and Hunter was a great big dog. There were three cats, a kitten, two rabbits, a goldfish, a guinea pig, Ross's rat Roly – and there were mice. There was a mousehole upstairs on the landing

and a mousehole downstairs in the hall. Tim and Tia had seen another big mousehole in the kitchen, but they never told anyone. They liked mice.

"Do you like mice?" Tia asked Mum.

"I rather think I do," said Mum. "Just as long as they don't get into my food cupboards. Or the vegetable rack."

"They could eat the brussels sprouts any time they like," said Ross. "I hate brussels sprouts."

"I love them!" said Tim. "It's cabbage I don't like."

"I do," said Ross. "I could eat cabbage for ever and ever."

"I don't mind cabbage sometimes," said Jason, "but I do like mice. I like them lots."

"Nice mice," said Daisy B.

"Dear little mice," said Tim. "Do you think they eat our crumbs?"

"Yes," said Tia. "They aren't like country mice. They can't find seeds and nuts and berries."

The smell began slowly. Mum noticed it first. She went round the kitchen looking in cupboards and in the fridge.

"Can you smell anything?" she asked Julius.

"I'm not sure," Julius said. "I think I can."

"Pooh!" said Ross. "I can! It smells like something mouldy."

"That's what I thought," said Mum.

The smell got worse.

Mum and Julius looked everywhere, but they couldn't find anything.

"Maybe it's a ghost!" said Tim.

"Ghosts don't smell, stupid," said Ross.

"Don't like it," said Daisy B.

"Yuck!" said Jason.

"Can't Tiny and Hunter sniff it out?" asked Tia.

"Yeah! Detective dogs!" said Tim.

Tiny and Hunter wagged their tails, but they didn't find anything that smelt nasty.

The smell got stronger still.

Even Granny Annie could smell it, right at the very top of the house.

"Whatever can we do?" Mum asked her.

Phew, what a smell!

"Maybe you should take up the floorboards," said Granny Annie.

"Oh dear," said Mum. "Do you think so?"

"I'll get my tools," said Julius. "We've got to do something."

Everyone stood round while Julius took up the first floorboard.

"Oh MY!" said Julius.

Under the floorboards was a strange, grey-green, dusty, musty collection of apple cores, biscuits, crusts of bread, bacon rinds, cheese … and something green and mushy. Something that smelt very strongly indeed.

"Phew!" said Julius. "That smells terrible!"

"Looks like a ghost's dinner!" said Ross.

"Wherever has all that food come from?" asked Mum. She looked round at the children. "Tia! Have you been putting food down the mousehole?"

Tia looked surprised. "Did you know there was a mousehole here?"

"Of course I did," said Mum. "Everyone knows!"

"Oh," said Tia. "I thought only me and Tim knew."

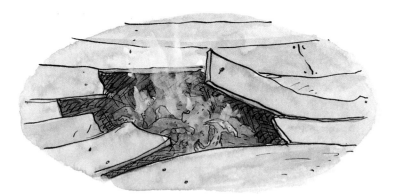

"I knew," said Jason. "I gave the mouse my crusts."

Daisy B nodded. "Nice mousey," she said. "Daisy B gives mousey biscuits."

Mum and Julius looked at Tia and Tim. "And what have you been feeding the mouse?"

"Only a few things," said Tia. "We gave it bits of bacon. And cheese. And apple cores."

Granny Annie began to laugh. "It's not surprising there's been a strange smell!" she said. "Even the hungriest little mouse couldn't have eaten all of that!"

"But what's that green mushy stuff?" asked Mum. "That smells worst of all."

No one said anything.

Then Ross coughed. "Um. Well. I thought they might like my brussels sprouts … "

"And I might have put a teeny tiny bit of cabbage down … " said Tim.

"No wonder it smells dreadful," said Mum. She looked sternly at the children. "No more food down the mousehole! Understand?"

Some time later, after a great deal of cleaning up, they all sat down for a cup of tea.

Granny Annie handed round a plate of biscuits. "I've been doing some thinking," she said. "Perhaps the mouse could have a little corn. Just now and then. And perhaps from now on Ross could eat Tim's cabbage. And Tim could eat Ross's brussels sprouts."

Ross and Tim beamed at her and then at each other.

"It's a deal!" they said.

*"I like those children," says Little Ghost. "Tell me more about that boy – what was his name? The one who said 'YUCK!'"*

*"Jason? I'll tell you a story about him next week," Big Ghost says and he floats off the vegetable rack and back up to the top of the cupboard. "Now, hurry home. It's time for your dinner."*

*Little Ghost wrinkles up his nose. "Hope it's not cabbage!" And he slips away out of the kitchen. "See you next week!" he calls as he goes, but Big Ghost doesn't hear. He's already asleep …*

# WEEK 3

*Another week has gone by, but this time Big Ghost is awake for once. He's hiding behind the coats in the hall. As Little Ghost bundles himself through the keyhole, Big Ghost pops out.*

*"BOO!"*

*Little Ghost jumps and giggles. "Got me!" he says.*

*"Are you ready for your story about Jason?" asks Big Ghost.*

*Little Ghost slides into a coat pocket. "Ready!"*

## Jason's Big Sticky Bun

Julius and Jason were out shopping.

They'd been to the dry cleaners and they'd been to the chemist.

"Right," said Julius, looking at his list. "We'll go to the library next. Then the fish shop. Then the supermarket."

"Can I have a big sticky bun?" Jason asked as they walked towards the library.

"No," said Julius. "Not today. We'll get some apples when we go to the supermarket – they're better for your teeth."

"Apples are boring," said Jason. "I'd much rather have a bun." And he began to kick an old Coke can along the pavement.

"Don't do that," said Julius.

Jason kicked the can into the gutter. "Why can't I have a bun?"

Julius sighed. "I told you – they're not good for your teeth. Besides, you won't eat your dinner if you have a bun now."

"I will," said Jason. "If I promise to eat every little bit of my dinner can I have a sticky bun?"

"No!" Julius said.

"Please please PLEASE can I have a bun?" wheedled Jason.

"Listen, Jason." Julius sounded cross. "Boys who nag don't get buns."

"So what sort of boys do get them?" Jason asked.

"Helpful ones," said Julius. "Boys who help carry bags. Boys who don't kick cans along the pavement. Boys who don't argue."

"Ah," said Jason and he was very quiet as he followed Julius up the steps into the library.

When Julius had checked in the old books Jason coughed politely.

"Excuse me, Julius. Shall I look after the bags while you choose the new books?"

Julius looked surprised. "What? Oh, OK. That would be great."

Jason sat patiently while Julius chose books for Tim and Tia and Daisy B.

"Are you feeling OK?" Julius asked.

"Yes, thank you," said Jason. "And I don't need to choose a book, thank you. I'm still reading my book on dinosaurs."

When they came out of the fish shop Jason took the bag without being asked.

He didn't ask for anything extra all the way round the supermarket.

He helped Julius pack the bags and then asked which ones he should carry.

"Jason," said Julius as they walked towards the car park, "you've been a real help today."

"Yes," said Jason. "I know. So can we go to the baker's for my big sticky bun now?"

Julius nearly dropped everything. "What did you say?"

"Well," said Jason, "you said boys who carried bags and didn't kick cans and were helpful got buns. I've done all that, haven't I?"

Julius groaned. "OK, Jason. You win. We'll get a bun on the way home. But you'd better eat every last mouthful of your dinner."

"Yes," said Jason. He grinned. "And I'll eat an apple too."

*"I like Jason," Little Ghost says. "He's clever!" He slithers out of the coat pocket and peers at a hole in the skirting board. "What's that hole?"*

*"A mousehole," says Big Ghost.*

*"Ooooo!" says Little Ghost. "I want a story about the mouse who lives in there!"*

*"Next week," says Big Ghost and he yawns. "I've got things to do."*

*"I know," sighs Little Ghost. "And I've got to go home. Bye! See you next week!"*

# WEEK 4

*Little Ghost has been counting. "One, two, three, four, five, six – seven days!" he says. "Tonight's the night for my mouse story!" And he nags and nags until Mama Ghost takes him to the big old house.*

*Big Ghost is hovering in the hall.*

*"Squeak squeak squeak!" calls Little Ghost. "I've come for my mouse story!"*

*Big Ghost stretches and then he nods. "I remember," he says. "I'll tell you what happened when two little country mice came here to stay."*

## When William and Mimi Came to Stay

Once there was a house and in the house there was a hallway. In the hallway was a mousehole and in the mousehole lived Ferdie and his mum. They lived a quiet life, so Ferdie was pleased to hear that his cousins were coming to stay.

"We can all play together!" he said.

Mum nodded. "Don't forget that William and Mimi are coming from the country. They'll be very quiet little mice. You must be sure to look after them."

Scritch … scritch … scritch.

There was a teeny weeny scratching on Ferdie's front door.

"Here they are!" shouted Ferdie. He ran to open the door, but before he got there –

BANG! BANG! BANG!

The door shook.

"Goodness me!" said Mum. "Whatever is that?"

Mum Mouse opened the front door, just a crack.

Ferdie peeped round her to see who was there – and saw two tiny mice standing on the doorstep.

"It's William and Mimi!" said Mum and she opened the door wide.

William scuttled in and hid behind the sofa.

Mimi stayed on the doorstep.

"HELLO!" she said.

Ferdie put his paws over his ears. Mimi had the loudest voice he had ever heard.

"GUESS WHAT?" Mimi went on in her loud loud voice. "WE'VE JUST SEEN A BIG FURRY ANIMAL WITH LONG WHITE WHISKERS. IT WAS ASLEEP ON THE DOORMAT. IT WENT PURRRRR!"

Mum Mouse pulled Mimi inside. Then she shut the door and locked it.

"Oh, Mimi!" she said. "That was the cat! Cats eat mice like you!"

"Oh … oh … oh … " wailed William from behind the sofa. "Aunty Mouse, please can we go home? I don't like it here!"

"Poor William," said Mum. She gave him a cuddle. "Don't worry – you're quite safe. And Ferdie will look after you when you go out."

William dived under a cushion. "But I don't want to go out," he wailed.

Mimi jumped up and down.

"OUT?" she boomed. "GOODY GOODY! CAN WE GO NOW?"

Ferdie was staring at Mimi. She really was a very tiny mouse.

"Was it you who went BANG BANG BANG on our door?" he asked.

"YES," Mimi said. "I THOUGHT YOU WOULDN'T HEAR US." She beamed at Mum Mouse. "WILLIAM'S THE QUIET ONE. I'M THE NOISY ONE."

Mum Mouse sat down rather hard on the sofa.

"Mum," said Ferdie, "shall we have some cheese?"

Ferdie and Mum Mouse had a nibble each.

William couldn't eat anything.

Mimi ate her nibble, William's nibble and all of the rest of the cheese on the plate.

"YUMMY!" Mimi said and wiped her whiskers.

"Mimi," said Mum Mouse, "er … how long are you staying for?"

"I think we should go home now," whispered William.

"WE CAN STAY FOR A WEEK," Mimi bellowed.

"Oh," said Mum Mouse. "How lovely."

That afternoon Mum Mouse had a headache.

"Shall I take Mimi and William out?" Ferdie suggested.

"That would be very kind, dear," said Mum. "Promise you'll be *very* careful."

"I promise," said Ferdie.

Mimi jumped up. "I'M READY!" she said. "COME ON, WILLIAM – "

Where are they off to?

But William wouldn't come. He said he'd rather do the dusting.

"And I'll make Aunty Mouse a cup of tea," he whispered.

"Thank you, dear," said Mum Mouse.

"SH," said Ferdie as he and Mimi tiptoed out of the mousehole.

CRASH!

Mimi slammed the front door behind her.

**"Meow?"** The cat woke up with a jump. Ferdie pushed Mimi under the hall cupboard.

The cat got up and stretched. Then it began sniffing up and down the hallway.

"I told you to be quiet!" Ferdie whispered crossly. "Now – don't move!"

Mimi nodded and the two little mice stayed very very still.

After two minutes they were chilly.

After three minutes they were cold.

After five minutes they were shivering.

"B'RRR," said Mimi.

"Shush!" said Ferdie.

At last the cat padded away.

"Phew!" said Ferdie. "Thank goodness!"

"CAN WE GO AND FIND SOME CHEESE NOW?" Mimi asked.

"No," Ferdie said, "we're going home." And he hurried out from under the cupboard. Mimi hurried after him – and stopped.

The big black cat was crouching in front of the mousehole. He was staring at Ferdie's front door without moving. Only his whiskers twitched.

Ferdie and Mimi stared. They could see the cat's claws … and they looked very sharp.

They could see his teeth … and they looked even sharper.

Suddenly the front door flew open. There was William, shaking a small yellow duster.

***"Atchooo!"*** the cat sneezed.

"Eeeeek!" William squeaked. He tried to run, but –

***"Meeow!"***

The cat pounced on his tail.

"Help!" yelled William. "Help!"

The cat hung on firmly.

Mimi let go of Ferdie's paw and rushed towards the cat. "LET GO OF MY BROTHER!" she boomed in her loudest voice. "LET HIM GO!"

*"Hisssss!"* The cat jumped and let go of William. William fell flat on his face. "YOU'RE A BIG BULLY!" roared Mimi.

The cat jumped round to look at her.

**"Merrow!"** he said. **"A big bully, eh? Well, well – never mind. Big bullies need big dinners. And you'll make a tasty little – YERROWWWWWWWWWWWWW!"**

The cat leapt in the air. Ferdie grabbed Mimi and bundled her through the door. William rushed after them. Ferdie shut the door with a SLAM.

Ferdie and Mimi stared at William.

William was picking fur out of his mouth.

"William!" said Ferdie. "Did you just bite the cat?"

William nodded.

"THAT'S MY BROTHER," said Mimi. "HE ALWAYS DOES THINGS SO QUIETLY … "

"Phew," said Ferdie. "Hey – William – are you still frightened of cats?"

"Yes," said William. He looked thoughtful. "But I don't think I'm very frightened. In fact, I might stay here a little longer." He put down his duster. "Now, I was just about to make some tea … "

*"That was a funny story!" says Little Ghost, clapping. "Was the cat Fat Freda?"*

*Big Ghost smiles. "I think it was," he says. "But that was a while ago. Fat Freda doesn't catch mice any more."*

*"Good," says Little Ghost. "I'm like Jason. I like mice." He slides off Big Ghost's knee and floats slowly towards the front door. "I don't suppose there's time … ?"*

*"NO," says Big Ghost. "Come back next week!"*

# WEEK 5

*As Little Ghost arrives at the house he sees Big Ghost sitting
on a flower pot in the garden.*

*"Time for a story about the garden," says Big Ghost.*

*"Would you like to hear about a slug who had a party?"*

*"Yes PLEASE," says Little Ghost.*

## Susie Slug's Happy Day

It was Susie Slug's birthday and she was very excited.

"Can I have a party?" she asked Mother Slug.

"I don't know, dear," said Mother Slug. "What's a party?"

"I heard about them at school," said Susie. "Betty Butterfly and Mary Moth have both had parties." She looked sad for a moment. "They didn't ask me, though. No one ever asks me to their party."

"No one's ever asked me to a party either," said Mother Slug. "Are they fun?"

"Oh yes!" said Susie. "You ask people to come to your house and they bring – what are those things called? Oh yes. Presents. They bring presents and you have nice things to eat and drink. Then they sing 'Happy Birthday to You' and you blow out the candles on your cake."

"Oh," said Mother Slug. "Well, I suppose we could try. There's never been any such thing as a party in my family, but there's no harm in trying something new."

Susie found a large lettuce leaf. She wrote: *"Susie Slug is having a Birthday Party at Teatime. Please come and bring presents. There will be nice things to eat ..."* She balanced the leaf on the top of a watering can so that everyone in the garden could see it and then hurried back home to help Mother Slug make cabbage crunchies.

News of Susie's party spread round the garden.

"A slug having a party!" Betty Butterfly fluttered her wings in astonishment. "How horrid! I certainly won't be going."

"Nor me," said little Mary Moth. She always did what Betty did.

"I like nice things to eat," said Stuart Snail, "but I haven't got a present, so I can't go."

*Susie Slug is having a Birthday Party at Teatime. Please come and bring presents. There will be nice things to eat...*

"Nor have I," said Clive Caterpillar. "Pity. I love cake."

"I don't want to go on my own," said Wallis Worm. "I'd be shy."

It was nearly teatime when Bertie Bee came buzzing down to look at the lettuce leaf. "A party!" he said. "What fun! Let's all go! Let's go now!"

"We can't," said Clive and Stuart. "We haven't got any presents."

"We don't want to," said Betty and Mary.

"I'm shy," said Wallis.

"Dear me," said Bertie and he buzzed away to see what was going on in Susie's part of the garden.

Susie was sitting on a cabbage stalk looking very sad. A tear was rolling down her silver nose and Bertie heard her sniff loudly. In front of her was a beautiful tea. Every leafy plate was decorated with buttercups. There was a huge, green leaf cake and on the top were four dandelion puff balls.

35

"Hello," said Bertie. "Is this where the party is?"

Susie nodded. "Yes," she said, "but nobody's come. I'm going to sing Happy Birthday to Me and then I'm going to blow out my candles and then I'm going to go to bed."

"Don't do that!" said Bertie. "I'm sure everybody will come soon."

"Do you really think so?" asked Susie, and she smiled a watery smile.

"I'll just go and show them the way," said Bertie. "Oh – can I ask you something? What sort of presents are you expecting?"

Susie shook her head. "I don't exactly know what presents are," she said, "but Betty Butterfly said she had them at her party last week. She told me that everyone has presents when it's their party. Mary said so too." Susie looked at Bertie Bee a little sideways. "But I heard Betty tell Mary that she had horrid dandelion toffee from Wallis and Stuart and Clive. She said it was all slimy and she hid it under a flower pot!"

"Did she?" said Bertie Bee. "Well I never. That's a very interesting thing to know."

"Oh, please don't tell Betty

I heard her!" said Susie. "She didn't see me." She sighed. "People often don't."

"Just give me ten minutes," said Bertie, "and they'll all be here for your party." He winked at Susie and zoomed off.

Betty Butterfly was showing Mary, Wallis, Stuart and Clive how lovely her wings looked when she sat in a sunbeam.

"You're so beautiful," said Mary and the others nodded.

"Indeed you are," said Bertie as he landed beside her. "And I heard you had a birthday last week."

Betty flapped her wings so that they shimmered. "Oh yes," she said. "Of course everybody brought me wonderful presents."

Mary, Wallis, Stuart and Clive smiled proudly.

"I have so many friends," Betty said and she sniffed. "Not like that slug."

"Funny you should mention Susie," said Bertie. "I was just about to ask if you were all ready to come to her party. She's waiting for you and there's a splendid tea. With cake. And – " Bertie stared very hard at Betty – "I'm sure she'd be thrilled with any kind of present at all. She's not the sort of

37

person who hides presents away under a flower pot."

Betty stopped flapping her wings. She looked at Bertie. Bertie winked.

"But we don't want to know about that sort of person, do we?" he said.

Betty blushed a very deep pink. Then she smiled her sweetest smile.

"But of course we're going to Susie's party. Aren't we, gang? We'll take her – " Betty waved an elegant leg in the air – "daisies!"

They each hurried off to pick a daisy.

"Good idea," said Bertie. "Now – let's go!"

And Betty and Mary and Bertie flew to Susie Slug's party, while Clive and Stuart and Wallis slithered as fast as they could in between the cabbage stalks …

I'm glad Susie had a nice birthday.

and Susie Slug had the best party ever.

What's more, the very next time there was a party (it was Wallis Worm's birthday) Susie Slug was invited and she brought the most delicious dandelion toffee that Betty Butterfly had ever tasted.

"Is dandelion toffee really nice?" asks Little Ghost.

"It is if you're a slug," says Big Ghost.

"Oh," says Little Ghost and he hurries away.

39

# WEEK 6

It's a cold, wet evening. Little Ghost wriggles through the keyhole as quickly as he can.

"Big Ghost!" he calls. "I'm here!"

There's no answer.

"Big Ghost!" wails Little Ghost. "Where are you?"

"Here I am!" says Big Ghost as he floats down through the ceiling. "Come up and see a friend of mine."

Little Ghost chases after Big Ghost and finds himself upstairs. Big Ghost is sitting on the stairs and a small fluffy kitten is curled up next to him, purring loudly.

"OH!" says Little Ghost. "He's lovely! What's his name?"

Big Ghost chuckles. "You'll have to find that out for yourself!" he says.

"Oooooh!" Little Ghost looks excited. "That'll be fun! Where did he come from?"

"I'll tell you the kitten's story," says Big Ghost. "But it's a long story. Tonight we'll begin with the first part."

Little Ghost snuggles up to the kitten. "I'm ready," he says.

It's time for kitten's story, are you sitting comfortably?

# The Kitten with no Name: Part One

Once there was a kitten without a name. He was born under a hedge, so he had no home either.

"Meeow," said his mother. "When you are big enough we will go out into the world. I'll take you somewhere very special where we can live happily ever after."

"How will we know when we've found the right place?" asked the kitten.

His mother began to purr. "We'll know," she said. "We'll feel warm and cosy and someone will love us."

"That sounds good," said the kitten and he snuggled into the dry leaves and went to sleep.

The kitten grew bigger. Every day he asked his mother if he was big enough to go out into the world and every day she said, "Not yet."

"We're going to find somewhere special where we can live happily ever after," said the kitten. "Aren't we, Mother?"

"That's right," said his mother. "Somewhere very special."

"Why is it special?" asked the kitten.

"Well," said his mother, "it'll be special because it'll be our very own home."

"Our own home!" the kitten said. "That sounds good. Will it keep out the wind and the rain?"

"It certainly will," his mother told him. "There'll be a roof and walls."

The kitten snuggled down against his mother's warm side. "Tell me again how we'll know the right place," he said.

"We'll feel warm and cosy," said his mother and she licked his ears.

"You've forgotten the best bit," said the kitten.

"Oh yes," said his mother. "And someone will love us. They'll love us very much."

"That's right," said the kitten and he began to purr.

"Purr … purr … purr … "

*"Go on," says Little Ghost. "What happened next?"*

*"That's the end of Part One," says Big Ghost. "I'll tell you some more another time. It's time for you to go now, Little Ghost."*

*Little Ghost strokes the kitten. "Goodbye," he says. "I'll see you soon. And I'll find out your name!"*

*The kitten purrs even louder and Little Ghost slips away.*

Turn to page 64 for the next kitten's story.

# WEEK 7

*It's a warm, dry night and Big Ghost is fast asleep in the apple tree. Little Ghost wakes him very gently.*

*"Ooooooooh!" he whispers. "I want my stooooooory!"*

*Big Ghost nods sleepily. "I'll tell you a story about the garden," he says. "Just a short one tonight – I'm very tired. I'll tell you a little story about Daisy B in the garden … "*

## Flowers for Mummy

Daisy B likes flowers.

Daisy B's mummy likes flowers too.

Daisy B goes into the garden. There are lots of flowers in the garden.

Daisy B is a clever girl. She knows red. Daisy B picks ALL the red flowers.

Look, Mummy!

Flowers for Mummy!

Mummy is cross.

Daisy B sits down to think.

Why is Mummy cross?

OH!

Daisy B knows why Mummy is cross. Mummy is cross because Mummy doesn't like red flowers. Mummy likes yellow flowers!

Daisy B is a clever girl. She knows yellow.

Daisy B goes into the garden.

Daisy B picks all the yellow flowers.

Now Mummy will be happy!

Look, Mummy!

Flowers for Mummy!

*Little Ghost laughs out loud. "She was naughty, wasn't she, Big Ghost?"*

*Big Ghost doesn't answer. He's asleep again.*

*Little Ghost floats away from the apple tree and looks at the flowers. They look silver in the moonlight. Would Mama Ghost like a silver flower, he wonders?*

*"Little Ghost!" Mama Ghost is waiting by the gate. "Little Ghost! What are you doing?"*

*Little Ghost jumps. "Nothing!" he says and floats towards her …*

# WEEK 8

*Mama Ghost and Little Ghost float over the roof of the big old house.*

*"I'm going to go down a chimney," Little Ghost whispers. "I'm going to give Big Ghost a surprise!"*

*WHEEEEEE! Little Ghost slides down, but Big Ghost is waiting by the fireplace.*

*"I heard you coming," he says and he laughs.*

*Little Ghost looks round in amazement. "Where are we?" he asks.*

*"It's the playroom," says Big Ghost. "Look, there are all the children's toys!"*

*Little Ghost whizzes down to have a closer look. "What funny-looking animals," he says. "What are they?"*

*Big Ghost picks up an animal with a long neck. "This is a giraffe. I'll tell you a giraffe story."*

## Why the Giraffe has a Long Neck

In the beginning of the beginning all the animals looked very much the same. The tigers didn't have stripes. The elephants didn't have trunks. The monkeys didn't climb trees and they certainly didn't have long tails. Even the giraffes looked very much the same as everyone else.

All the animals lived in the great green forest and all the animals were friends. The elephants and the monkeys played hide and seek all day. The tigers and the hippos went on picnics together. The lions and the crocodiles told each other stories.

The giraffes were too shy to play hide and seek or to go on picnics, but they enjoyed watching the other animals. Sometimes when they were feeling very brave they would play Grandmother's Footsteps because they were very good at being quiet.

Every day in the forest was like the very best sort of holiday.

But then it rained. It rained and it rained and it rained and it rained. The animals began to worry that the forest would turn into a huge lake and they all met to decide what they should do.

"We're going to grow long noses so that we can breathe even when we're under water," said the elephants.

"We're going to learn how to climb the trees so the water won't reach us," said the monkeys. "And we're going to grow long tails so we don't fall off the branches."

"We are going to grow golden fur so that we can hide away in the sandy deserts," said the lions. "It doesn't rain in the sandy deserts."

"We're going to grow stripes," said the tigers. "We're going to live among the grasses and the bushes beyond the great green forest and the lake."

"We're going to learn to swim," said the hippos.

"We're going to learn to swim too," said the crocodiles. "Then we won't mind if the whole world is a lake."

The giraffes thought the other animals were very clever.

"What shall we do?" they asked each other, but no one had any clever ideas. Some giraffes thought they should grow trunks like the elephants. Some thought they should climb trees like the monkeys. Some thought they should follow the lions into the deserts. Some thought they should learn to swim. They simply couldn't make up their minds.

"Let's not decide just yet," said the oldest giraffe. "We'll wait and watch and we'll see what happens to the others."

So the giraffes began to wait and watch. They stood on their tippy toes so they could peer over bushes and they stretched up and up to peep through the branches of the trees. They stretched up and up to squint over the long grasses and they stood on their tippy toes to peek through the hanging vines.

"The elephants have grown long noses!" they said to each other. "Do we want long noses?"

"Looks odd to me," said the oldest giraffe. "Let's keep watching."

"Ooooh!" said a little giraffe. "I can see the hippos and the crocodiles swimming!"

"Looks chilly in that water," said the oldest giraffe. "Let's keep watching."

"The lions are yellow! The tigers are stripy!"

"I'm not impressed," said the oldest giraffe. "Let's keep watching."

"Oooh! Look at the monkeys! They can swing from tree to tree!"

"No no no," said the oldest giraffe. "I don't fancy swinging from trees at all. Let's keep –"

"Look look LOOK!" said the little giraffe.

"What at?" asked the oldest giraffe. "Haven't we seen all the other animals and their funny little ways?"

"No!" said the little giraffe. "Look at US! We've all grown long legs! And long necks!"

The oldest giraffe looked around. The little giraffe was quite right. All the giraffes had long legs and long necks.

"H'm," he said. "I'd say we look rather splendid. I suggest we stay just the way we are."

"And if there is a flood," said the little giraffe, "we'll be too tall to drown."

"Of course we will," said the oldest giraffe. "I was just about to mention that."

So all the giraffes kept their long long necks … even though the forest never did turn into a huge lake.

*"And they've still got long necks," says Little Ghost.*

*"So they have," says Big Ghost and he puts the giraffe back on the floor.*

*"This is a nice room," says Little Ghost. "There are lots of things here to tell stories about."*

*"There certainly are," Big Ghost agrees.*

*"Ooooooooooo!"*

*Little Ghost giggles. "That's Mama Ghost wailing down the chimney! I'd better go. But I'll come again next week!"*

# WEEK 9

Big Ghost is wondering if Little Ghost has forgotten about his story. It's getting late and there's no sign of him.

Oh! There he is!

"I'm sorry I'm late," he puffs. "Grandma Ghost is staying with us. Mama says I mustn't stay long."

"We'll have a short story, then," says Big Ghost. "A spider story!"

## Fly Pie

Here I am
In my web
In the corner
By the light
On the ceiling
And I'm watching.
And I'm spying.
What do I spy?
I spy a fly.
Buzz buzz buzz ...

Watch out, fly!

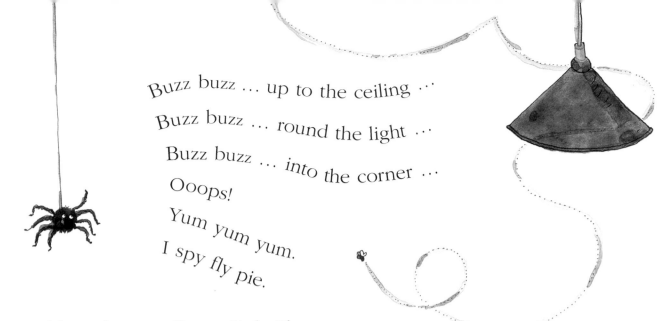

Buzz buzz ... up to the ceiling ...
Buzz buzz ... round the light ...
Buzz buzz ... into the corner ...
Ooops!
Yum yum yum.
I spy fly pie.

"I know why you told me that story!" says Little Ghost.

"Do you?" asks Big Ghost.

"Yes! There's a big spider up there in the corner!" Little Ghost says. "Can I have another spider story?"

"Another time," says Big Ghost. "Your grandma's waiting. Off you go!"

# WEEK 10

*"Hi!" Little Ghost says. "I'm back! And you haven't told me about any of the children for ages!"*

*"Haven't I?" says Big Ghost. "Dear me. Well, why don't I tell you about Tia and her birthday party?"*

## Tia's Birthday Party

"I'm having a party, I'm having a party, I'm having a party!" Tia danced round and round the room. "It's my turn today!"

"Not another party!" said Teddy. "Didn't you all go bowling last weekend for your birthday?"

"That was Tim's party," said Tia. "And he only asked boys. Mum said I could have my own party this weekend and I'm having girls. Girls are much the best, Teddy."

"Oh," said Teddy. "I see."

Tia did another twirl and fell over. She rubbed her head. "I'm going to have a pink bow in my hair. You can have a bow round your neck, Teddy."

Teddy snorted. "No thank you."

"Don't you like birthday parties?" Tia asked.

Ooo I like parties.

53

Teddy thought about it. "I don't think I do. You cried last week when you got back from bowling."

"I won't cry at MY party," said Tia. "Even if I don't win anything."

"Even if you don't win pass the parcel?"

"No," said Tia firmly. "I'm too big to cry."

"Um," said Teddy.

Tia went upstairs to the bathroom.

"Don't forget to wash your ears," Teddy said.

Tia began to look very soapy.

"I always wash my ears." She gave Teddy a thoughtful stare. "You don't look very clean, Teddy."

"If you don't hurry up," Teddy said quickly, "you won't be ready on time."

Tia squeezed out her sponge. She peered at herself in the mirror. "I'll look pretty with a pink bow."

"Um," said Teddy.

"Claudia's wearing a pink bow too. She says if her best friend is wearing a bow, she's got to wear one to be the same. Claudia says best friends always wear the same things. And Emmie's wearing the same as Cathy 'cos she's Cathy's best friend, but Kim's going to wear her dungarees." Tia stopped to giggle. "Kim hates bows."

Teddy was counting. He was finding it very difficult beause he only had four paws. "How many people are coming to the party?" he asked.

"Five," said Tia. She put down the towel. "I wanted ten but Mum said that was too many."

Teddy started counting all over again. "Wait a minute," he said. "Claudia and Claudia's best friend with the bow and Emmie and Cathy and Kim. And you haven't counted YOU. That makes six."

Tia was pulling her party dress over her head. She came out looking hot and bothered.

"What did you say? I couldn't hear."

"You've got six people coming to your party," Teddy said.

"Are you sure?" Tia asked.

Ooo, dear! What is Tia doing?

Teddy counted again. "Yes. It's six. And you told Mum five."

Tia shook her head. "Oh dear," she said. "And they'll be here in a minute."

Mum wasn't very pleased.

She did the zip up on the back of Tia's dress with a little *f'tttt* noise.

"Oh, Tia!" she said. "We've got five party hats and five crackers and five going home presents. Whatever can we do?"

Tia stood on one leg and looked anxious.

"We'll have to lay another place at the table," said Mum, "and you'll have to give away your party hat and cracker and going home present."

Teddy looked at Tia. Her chin was very wobbly and she was staring at the floor. "Can't I even have my going home pencil with the little dangly rubber?" she asked.

"No." Mum still sounded cross. "You said four children were coming. That's five with you. Now there's six."

Tia went into the sitting room. She sat down on the floor next to the basket with the going home presents. She put out her hand and patted one of the parcels. "It's a very special pencil," she said sadly. "I chose it myself."

"Ah," said Teddy.

Tia began to sniff. "It's the loveliest pencil I ever had," she said.

"I thought you were too old," said Teddy.

"Too old for what?"

"Too old to cry."

"It's not my party yet," said Tia crossly. "I can cry now if I want to."

Ross came bouncing into the sitting room. He was carrying a bunch of little labels. "Mum says we'll have to change the names on the going home parcels," he said cheerfully.

"Oh," said Tia.

"Go on, then," said Tim. "Who's coming?"

"Emmie," said Tia. "And Cathy. And Kim. And Claudia."

Ross turned over the five parcels. "That's right," he said. "And one for you. So who's the other kid?"

"What other kid?" asked Tia.

"Mum said you said there were SIX for your party."

Tia looked at Teddy. Teddy nodded.

"Claudia's best friend with the pink bow," he hissed.

"What friend?" said Tia.

Teddy sighed loudly. "You said Claudia was wearing a pink bow like her best friend."

Tia stared at Teddy. "But that's me!" she said. "I'M Claudia's best friend!"

"TIA!" said Ross. "Stop talking to that bear and TELL me about the presents!"

Tia began to giggle. She jumped up and did a huge twirl round and round the sitting room. "It's OK," she said. "It's only five after all. Teddy can't count!"

Teddy went to sit behind the basket as Tia rushed out to tell Mum that everything was all right.

"Anyone can make a mistake," he said to himself. "I just – er – got a little muddled." And he settled down to watch the party.

*"I like parties," says Little Ghost. "Have you ever been to a party, Big Ghost?"*

*"A very long time ago," says Big Ghost. "When I was a little ghost."*

*"Like me?" Little Ghost asks.*

*"That's right," says Big Ghost. "And now it's time for you to fly away home."*

# WEEK 11

*The moon is very bright tonight.*

*Big Ghost is outside, sitting on top of a rabbit hutch, and Little Ghost is flying round and round in circles above his head.*

*"Big Ghost! Big Ghost!" he says. "Is that a cage? What's inside it?"*

*"It's a rabbit," Big Ghost says. "This is Flopsy – Fluffy is in the hutch over there. Flopsy belongs to Tim and Fluffy belongs to Tia."*

*Little Ghost peeps into the hutch. "Flopsy's nose is twitching! Big Ghost – will you tell me a story about rabbits? Please?"*

*"Sit yourself down and I'll tell you about Middle Rabbit," says Big Ghost.*

## Middle Rabbit and the Cabbage Field

Big Rabbit, Middle Rabbit and Baby Rabbit lived with their grandma and grandpa in a burrow.

Big Rabbit was big enough to go to the cabbage field on his own, but Middle Rabbit and Baby Rabbit were not.

"But I am big," said Middle Rabbit. "I'm much bigger than Baby Rabbit."

"You're not big enough to go out alone," said Grandpa. "Eat your carrots and you'll soon grow."

Middle Rabbit ate his carrots. "Am I big enough now?" he asked.

"Not quite big enough," said Grandma. "Eat your lettuce and you'll soon grow."

Middle Rabbit ate his lettuce. "Am I big enough now?" he asked.

"No," said Big Rabbit. "You're not as big as me. When you're as big as me then you can go to the cabbage field on your own."

"Oh," said Middle Rabbit.

Middle Rabbit ate his cabbage. He ate his celery tops. He ate his parsnips. He ate his turnips.

He hurried off to see if he was as big as Big Rabbit. "Am I as big as you now?" he asked.

Big Rabbit patted Middle Rabbit's head. "No," he said. "I'm still bigger than you."

Middle Rabbit ate his beetroot. He ate his onions. He ate his radishes. He even ate his spinach.

He ran to see if he was as big as Big Rabbit. "Am I as big as you now?" he asked.

Big Rabbit pulled Middle Rabbit's ears. "No," he said. "I'm still bigger than you."

"Bother," said Middle Rabbit and he went to sit under a tree root.

Baby Rabbit followed him.

"It's no good," Middle Rabbit told Baby Rabbit. "I'll never be as big as Big Rabbit."

Baby Rabbit patted Middle Rabbit's paw. POP!

It was Mole. His little pink snout came popping out of a hole in the ground.

"Hello, Mole," said Middle Rabbit.

"Hello, Mole," said Baby Rabbit.

Mole pulled himself out of his hole.

"Why, hello, Big Rabbit," he said. "And hello to you too, Middle Rabbit."

Middle Rabbit looked round. He couldn't see Big Rabbit anywhere.

"Where's Big Rabbit?" he asked.

"You are," said Mole. "Aren't you?"

"No," said Middle Rabbit. "I'm Middle Rabbit."

"And I'm Baby Rabbit," said Baby Rabbit.

Mole sat down and stared at them. "Goodness me," he said. "I was sure you were Big Rabbit and Middle Rabbit." He laughed. "Oh silly me! It's because I haven't seen you for a long time. You must have grown."

Middle Rabbit looked at Baby Rabbit. Baby Rabbit looked at Middle Rabbit.

"Have we?" they asked.

Mole laughed again. "Indeed you have!"

"Oh!" said the rabbits. "Thank you, Mole!" And they went hopping and skipping back to their burrow.

"Grandma! Grandpa! Big Rabbit!" said Middle Rabbit. "Mole says we've grown! Mole thought I was Big Rabbit! Can I go to the cabbage field on my own now?"

"But you're still smaller than me," said Big Rabbit.

Grandpa smiled. "Middle Rabbit will always be smaller than you, Big Rabbit – until you're both quite grown up. He grows – but you do too!"

"Oh!" said Middle Rabbit.

Grandma looked at Middle Rabbit. "You're quite right," she said. "We didn't notice. You are a fine big rabbit. Tomorrow you can go to the cabbage field all on your own."

"Hurrah!" said Middle Rabbit and he danced round and round.

"And can I go on my own as well?" asked Baby Rabbit. "Mole thought I was Middle Rabbit!"

"You're not quite big enough yet to go out alone," said Grandpa.

"No," said Grandma. "Eat your carrots and you'll soon grow."

"Oh," said Baby Rabbit and his ears drooped.

Middle Rabbit looked at Baby Rabbit. There was a tear on the end of Baby Rabbit's whiskers.

"I'll go to the cabbage field on my own tomorrow," Middle Rabbit said, "because I am a fine big rabbit and that's what fine big rabbits do. But I might be lonely if I go on my own every day." He patted Baby Rabbit's paw and looked at Grandpa and Grandma. "Is Baby Rabbit big enough to go to the cabbage field with me?" he asked. "Then he won't be on his own – and I won't be either."

"I'll eat my spinach!" said Baby Rabbit.

And Grandpa and Grandma said yes.

*"Is Flopsy the rabbit in the story?" asks Little Ghost.*
*"Is he Middle Rabbit?"*

*Big Ghost chuckles. "He just might be, Little Ghost. He just might be. Now, I don't want to hurry you –"*

*Little Ghost sighs. "I know. It's past my bedtime. Bye, Big Ghost!"*

# WEEK 12

*"Coooeee!"* Little Ghost slithers down the kitchen chimney and arrives in the kitchen fireplace in a rush. The small fluffy kitten jumps up from the mat with a startled *"Miaow!"*

*"Sorry,"* says Little Ghost. *"You're the kitten without a name, aren't you? I do so want to hear some more about what happened to you … "*

*"That's a good idea,"* says Big Ghost as he floats over from the top of the cupboard. *"I'll tell you the next part of the kitten's story."*

## The Kitten with no Name: Part Two

Every day the kitten with no name scrambled out from his home under the hedge to play with the waving buttercups and to catch the dancing daisies. Every day he chased the butterflies that went flittering past.

"Be careful," said his mother. "Don't go too far."

"I'll be careful," said the kitten.

One day the kitten found an old conker. He patted it and it skittered across the ground. The kitten bounced after it – straight into a group of children who were on their way to the park nearby.

"Oh!" said a tall boy. "Look! What a pretty kitten!" And he picked the kitten up and hugged him.

"H'm," thought the kitten. "Being hugged is good. I've never been hugged before."

He began to purr loudly. PURR! PURR! PURR!

"Want to see the kitty!" said a very little girl.

The tall boy held the kitten out for her to see.

"Pretty kitty!" said the little girl. "Take him home?"

"No, Daisy B," said the tall boy. "We've already got Fat Freda and Big Tom and there's Granny Annie's Kitty Purr too – there's no room for another cat."

The very little girl began to cry.

"Want the kitty! Daisy B wants the kitty! Daisy B wants a kitty of her very own!"

"Come on," said the tall boy and he put the kitten down. "Let's go to the park – I'll push you on the swings."

"YES!" shouted the very little girl. She turned to wave to the kitten.

"Bye bye, pretty kitty. See you soon." And all the children ran off.

The kitten ran to his home under the hedge. "Mother," he said, "I was hugged!"

"Hugging is good if it isn't too tight," said his mother.

"It wasn't too tight," the kitten said. "It was nice. And a little girl wanted to take me home!"

His mother jumped to her feet and her fur bristled. "You must NEVER let anyone take you home," she said. "We're going to go to our own home!"

"I know," said the kitten. "And it will be warm and cosy and someone will love us."

"That's right," said his mother.

The kitten looked hopeful. "Will we be hugged?"

"Of course," said his mother. "Now wash your paws and whiskers and I'll tuck you up."

The kitten curled up in his little leafy bed. "I think," he said sleepily, "I shall dream about being hugged." And he shut his eyes and began to purr.

Turn to page 91 for the next part of kitten's story.

*"OH!" says Little Ghost, his eyes shining. "The kitten met the children who live in this house!"*

*"That's right," says Big Ghost.*

*"So how did he get here?" asks Little Ghost.*

*"I'll tell you about that another time," says Big Ghost and he yawns a huge yawn. "I'll see you next week, Little Ghost."*

*Little Ghost nods. "Thank you, Big Ghost."*

# WEEK 13

*It's a windy night. Little Ghost laughs and laughs as he blows round the old house and in through the keyhole of the big front door.*

*"Woooooo! Woooooo!" he calls. "Here I am, Big Ghost!"*

*Big Ghost settles himself and Little Ghost on a pile of books in the hall.*

*"I'll tell you a story about a windy day like this," he says.*

## Windy Thursday

There was once a Thursday when the wind blew … and blew … and blew …

The weathercock twirled round and round until he was dizzy. Doors banged. Windows rattled and Jason's favourite T-shirt blew off the washing line and ended up in a blackberry bush.

"B'rrrr!" said Granny Annie. "It's cold! Come inside and shut the door."

"B'rrrr!" said Mum. "Let's light the fire!"

"B'rrrr!" said Ross. "Can we have hot chocolate?"

"Oooh yes!" said Tia and Tim.

"Me too!" said Jason.

"Me!" said Daisy B.

Granny Annie made hot chocolate for everyone while Mum lit the kitchen fire.

"Atchoo!" sneezed Ross. "It's very smoky!"

"It's the wind," said Mum, as Ross sneezed again and again. "It's blowing like a grampus down the chimney."

"Is it?" Jason looked very surprised.

"Can't you see the smoke?" said Ross. "Atchoo!" He sneezed even louder.

Jason went a little closer to the fire. "What's it look like? And when's it coming?" he asked.

"Whatever are you talking about, Jason?" asked Granny Annie.

"The – what was it you said, Mum?" Jason said. "Oh – I remember. The grampus thing. The grampus the wind's blowing down the chimney."

Mum laughed. "Oh, Jason!"

"It's not blowing anything down the chimney, silly," Ross said. "Mum said the wind was blowing like a grampus. That's a great big

Brrr, Brrr!

animal like a seal and it blows – oh, bother –
ATCHOOOOO!"

"Ross!" Mum said. "Where's your hankie?"
And then she sneezed too. "Atchoo!
Atchoo! ATCHOO!"

"This fire's terrible!" said Granny
Annie and she pushed at the
coals with the poker. Another
cloud of smoke swirled around
the kitchen and Tia and Tim began
to sneeze as well. Daisy B held her
nose and Granny Annie flapped at
the smoke with a tea towel and
sneezed the loudest sneeze of all.

"ATCHOOOO!"

Jason began to giggle. "I know what the wind's
blowing down the chimney," he said. "It's blowing grampus sneezes!"

*"Atchoo!" says Little Ghost. "I can do it too! Atchoo!"*

*"Maybe you could sneeze yourself out through the keyhole?" says Big Ghost.*

*"Yes!" Little Ghost jumps up. "And blow all the way*
*home on the wind … "*

"*Look! It's me!*" *Little Ghost has found an open window in the old house. He floats inside and finds Big Ghost blowing gently at a butterfly on the sitting room curtains.*

"*It's got lost,*" *says Big Ghost.* "*It should be outside.*"

"*Tell me a story about a butterfly!*" *says Little Ghost.*

## Flutterby Butterfly

Flitter flutter! Flitter flutter! Flitter flutter!

Once I wasn't a beautiful flittery fluttery butterfly flying over the garden. Once I was – *guess what?*

An egg. A little tiny egg on the underside of a leaf.

I wriggled and crawled and crept out of the egg and I was – *guess what?*

A caterpillar! A little green caterpillar.

I munched and I crunched and I crunched and I munched and I grew and I grew until I was so fat that my outside skin split and I was – *guess what?*

Ho ho! Caught you out!

A BIGGER caterpillar with a

brand new skin!

I munched and I crunched

and I crunched and I munched

and I grew and I grew until I was so fat that my outside

skin split and I was – *guess what?*

A BIGGER caterpillar with a brand new skin!

I munched and I crunched and I crunched and I munched and I

grew and I grew until I was so fat that my outside skin split and I was –

*guess what?*

A BIGGER caterpillar with a brand new skin!

I munched and I crunched and I crunched and I munched and

I grew and I grew until I was so fat that my outside skin split

and I was – *guess what?*

My, he does look big.

A CHRYSALIS! With a hard brown case to keep me safe …

and I did nothing at all for ten long days …

and then my hard brown case split and I was –
*guess what?*

Yes! A flittery fluttery butterfly!

*"Do caterpillars go on eating all night?" Little Ghost asks.*

*"H'm," says Big Ghost. "I don't know. I expect they have a little snooze.*

*It's time that you went home."*

*"That was a short story," says Little Ghost, "but I did like it."*

*"I'll tell you a longer one next week," says Big Ghost.*

*"Promise?" says Little Ghost.*

*"Promise," says Big Ghost.*

# WEEK 15

*Little Ghost shimmers into the old house kitchen and finds one of the dogs still awake and munching dog biscuits.*

*"Oooooooh!" says Little Ghost and hides behind a saucepan.*

*Big Ghost yawns and wanders out from underneath the ironing board. "It's all right," he says. "Hunter won't hurt you. In fact, I was going to tell you a story about him."*

*"A long story?" asks Little Ghost and he tiptoes out.*

*"A long story," says Big Ghost.*

## Hunter's Lost Bone

Once there was a dog called Hunter. He lived in a big house with lots of children.

*"I know!" says Little Ghost. "Ross and Tim and Tia and Jason and Daisy B!"*

*"That's right," says Big Ghost. "Now, shush — and listen!"*

One day Hunter lost his bone. He took it out to the garden and buried it and then he couldn't find it again.

"Woof," he said. "Perhaps it's under the rose bush?"

He dug a big hole under the rose bush, but his bone wasn't there.

"Woof," he said. "Maybe it's underneath those little blue flowers?"

He dug an even bigger hole in the middle of the little blue flowers, but his bone wasn't there either.

"Woof," he said. "I know! It's under those little green leafy things." And he dug the biggest hole of all right in the middle of the little green leafy things, but there was still no sign of his bone.

"Ah," said Hunter and he sat down and scratched his ear. "Wherever could my bone be?"

"AAAAGH!"

There was a very loud noise. Mum had come out of the house and she had seen the holes in the garden.

"Hunter!" shouted Mum. "You are a very BAD dog! Just look at my garden! It looks dreadful! And my poor plants – you've ruined them!"

Hunter hung his head. He hadn't meant to spoil the garden. He was only looking for his bone.

"Go into the house at once!" Mum was still shouting. "And you are never to come out here again!"

Hunter went slowly into the house. He was very sad. He liked playing in the garden. Ross and Tim and Tia and Jason and Daisy B threw balls for him to chase and that was fun. Sometimes the next door cat came into the garden and made rude hissing noises and Hunter woofed and growled and chased it away and that was fun too. When the weather was hot he liked lying in the sunshine underneath the apple tree. It was a lovely garden and he would miss it … and he would never be able to find his bone.

That night Hunter had to sleep in the kitchen. Usually he slept on the end of Tim's bed, but Mum said he couldn't. She said he was a bad dog and he had to learn how to behave. Hunter wagged his tail, but Mum didn't understand that he was very sorry. Tim was sad too and he asked Mum PLEASE to let Hunter stay, but Mum still said no. Hunter had to learn to be a good dog, Mum said, and she put him in the kitchen and shut the door.

Oooo, look what Hunter's done.

77

That night Hunter couldn't get to sleep. The clock ticked very loudly. Fat Freda and Big Tom came in through the cat flap and they laughed at him.

"You've been put in here?" they said. "Ooh! What a bad dog!"

Hunter curled up into a ball and pretended to take no notice.

It was very very late when there was a scraping noise outside.

The back door slowly opened …

A torch beam flashed …

And two men came tiptoeing into the kitchen.

Hunter sat up and stretched and the men froze.

"Er … good dog," said one.

"You said the dog didn't sleep in the kitchen!" said the other.

Hunter wagged his tail.

"He looks harmless enough," said the first man.

Hunter wagged his tail harder.

"Yeah – reckon you're right," said the other. "Let's get on with it!"

The two men tiptoed past Hunter and opened the door into the hallway.

Hunter scratched, turned round in his basket – and then – **KERBOOM!** Hunter had a brilliant idea.

The back door was open – he could have one last look for his bone! He bounced out of the door, and **CRASH!** The two bicycles outside fell over. Hunter's ears flattened and he shot back into the kitchen just as the men came running out.

**BUMP! THUMP!**

The men fell over Hunter and said a great many very rude words that Hunter had never heard before. They scrambled up and made a wild dash for the garden as Julius and Mum came rushing into the kitchen –

**OUCH! OW! OUCH!**

There was a loud wailing noise from outside.

"My leg! My leg!" wailed one voice.

"My head! My head!" wailed the other.

Julius grabbed a torch, while Mum hurried to the telephone. All the children came tumbling into the kitchen.

"Nine, nine, nine – police, please!" Mum said. "My dog has caught two burglars!"

Hunter didn't quite understand what happened next. A car load of blue-uniformed men and women came roaring up and they found the two burglars in Mum's garden. They had fallen into the biggest of Hunter's holes and were covered in bumps and bruises. One of them had a bag and the bag was full of Mum's glittery rings and things. The police took both the burglars away.

Hunter didn't quite understand the next thing that happened either. All of a sudden he was patted and petted and told he was wonderful. All of a sudden he was a very GOOD dog. Then, slowly, everyone went back to bed.

Hunter scratched his ears and made himself comfortable on the end of Tim's blanket. Human beings were odd, he thought. Not sensible, like dogs. Still, if Mum thought he was a very good dog now, maybe she would let him into the garden tomorrow. He'd just remembered something very important. He was almost sure that his bone was under the tall yellow flowers by the greenhouse …

*"Did Hunter dig up the garden AGAIN?" Little Ghost wants to know.*

*"I think," Big Ghost says, "Mum gave him another bone."*

*"Good!" says Little Ghost and he slides off the ironing board. "Good night, Big Ghost."*

# WEEK 16

*Big Ghost is sitting on the top of a chimney pot. "Hello," he says as Little Ghost flutters up. "I was looking at the moon."*

*"There's another moon down there in the garden," says Little Ghost. "Look!"*

*"That's a football," Big Ghost says. "Sit down and I'll tell you a football story."*

## Daisy B and the Football

Daisy B wants to play football with Jason.

"You're too little," says Jason.

"Not little," says Daisy B.

"You are," says Jason and he kicks the football over the grass.

"Waaaaaaah!" Daisy B begins to cry.

"Daisy B," says Mum, "come and help me water the flowers."

"Flowers," says Daisy B and she goes with Mum to fetch the watering can.

Jason goes too.

"Why do flowers want water?" he asks.

"Flowers need sunshine and water to make them grow," Mum tells him.

"Oh," says Jason.

Jason goes back to playing football.

Mum finishes watering the flowers and goes back to the house.

Daisy B watches Jason.

"Daisy B play too," she says. "Please?"

Jason has an idea.

Jason thinks it's a very good idea.

"Shall I make you grow, Daisy B?" he asks.

Daisy B smiles her biggest smile.

"YES!" she says. "Make Daisy B grow!"

"WAAAAAAAAAAAAH!"

Daisy B goes running into the house.

Daisy B is VERY wet.

"DAISY!" says Mum. "Whatever have you been doing?"

"She wanted to play with me," says Jason. "She wanted to play football, but she's too little. She wanted to grow, so I watered her."

*Little Ghost looks down at the garden, shining silver in the moonlight. "Are those more footballs over there?" he asks.*

*"Those are cabbages," Big Ghost tells him. "I'll tell you a story about a disappearing cabbage next week, if you like."*

*"Yes PLEASE," says Little Ghost. "Oooooh, there's my mama!"*

*And he flies up above the chimney pots.*

# WEEK 17

*It's a clear and moonlit night. Little Ghost waves goodbye to Mama Ghost and floats down to land neatly on the top of a chimney pot, where Big Ghost is waiting for him.*

*"You said you'd tell me a story about a cabbage," Little Ghost reminds him.*

*"I hadn't forgotten," says Big Ghost.*

## Stuart Snail's Busy Day

One morning Stuart Snail woke up late. He knew it was late because the sun was high in the sky and his flower pot felt warm. He popped his head out of his shell and yawned … and then stared.

His cabbage was gone. His favourite cabbage, his breakfast, dinner and treat time cabbage, wasn't there any more. There was a hole in the ground and a scattering of earth – but that was all.

Stuart slithered down from his flower pot and went to investigate. There were footprints – big footprints. Human footprints. But no cabbage – and then Stuart had a terrible thought.

*Where was Susie Slug?*

84

Stuart and Susie had had a large cabbage supper the night before and Stuart was almost certain that Susie had said she wasn't going to go home. Susie had said she was much too full and she was just going to curl up and go home in the morning. But where was she now?

Stuart gulped. "Maybe she changed her mind and went home after all," he said to himself and he zoomed off in between the brussels sprouts and the lettuces as fast as he could go.

Susie's mother was shaking out the doormat when Stuart came panting up.

"Good morning, Stuart!" she said cheerfully. "Is Susie with you?"

"Er … no," Stuart said. He didn't know what to say. "Er … I think she must be asleep."

"Wake her up for me, there's a good snail," said Mrs Slug. "It's time she was home."

"Er … yes," said Stuart and he slithered away.

"I must find that cabbage!" he thought. "Where on earth could it have gone? Oh dearie dearie me – what can I do?"

"Hi, Stuart!" It was Bertie Bee buzzing cheerfully by. "How are you this lovely morning?"

"Oh Bertie!" said Stuart. "A terrible terrible thing has happened. Susie Slug went to sleep in my cabbage last night and now the cabbage has gone and Susie must have gone with it! And there are human footprints all over the place – and I don't know what to do!"

Bertie looked worried. "Oh dear," he said. "I do hope the humans haven't taken the cabbage to cut up and cook for their dinner."

"WHAT?" said Stuart. "Oh no! You don't mean … oh! oh! Oh, Bertie!" And Stuart fanned himself with a lettuce leaf in horror.

Bertie began to buzz faster. "We must get busy," he said. "We must save Susie! I'll fly over to the house and see if there's a cabbage in the kitchen. You go and look all over the garden. After all, Susie might have crawled out of the cabbage before it was taken."

Bertie buzzed away and Stuart went rushing off to see if Susie was having a little snack of newly planted radishes.

Susie wasn't there, but Wallis Worm was. He was practising his worm wheelies.

"Wallis!" said Stuart. "Have you seen Susie anywhere?"

Wallis shook his head. "Not today," he said. "Why?"

Stuart told Wallis the dreadful news.

"Sometimes the humans throw cabbages on the compost heap," Wallis said. "I've seen them there when I'm doing my burrowing and digging."

"Brilliant idea!" said Stuart and he and Wallis went slithering and wriggling off to the compost heap.

There was no sign of a cabbage, or Susie, but Betty Butterfly was there. She was fluttering above a heap of half dead flowers.

"Betty!" said Stuart. "Have you seen Susie anywhere?"

"No," said Betty. "Don't you think my wings look lovely next to these roses?"

"Oh, Betty," Stuart said. "Something awful has happened!" And he told Betty about the missing cabbage.

Betty stopped fluttering and started thinking.

"I've seen cabbages in the guinea pig's hutch," she said. "And the rabbits eat cabbage too."

"Quick!" shouted Stuart. "Let's go and see!" And he and Wallis and Betty went slithering and wriggling and fluttering to the hutch.

"Zzzzzzzz!" It was Bertie Bee. He came flying down as Stuart and Wallis puffed their way past the rabbit run.

"Good news!" Bertie said. "There's no sign of any cabbage in the kitchen. They've got carrots and beans and lettuce – but no cabbage."

"Hurrah!" said Wallis, but Stuart was looking at Betty. She was flapping her wings and waving wildly from the top of the hutch.

"I can see a cabbage!" she called.

"What's going on?" said a voice and Clive Caterpillar popped out from a clump of stinging nettles.

"It's Susie," said Stuart. "Someone picked my cabbage and Susie was in it!"

"And she might be in the guinea pig hutch," said Wallis anxiously.

"And the guinea pig might eat her!" said Stuart and he blew his nose loudly.

"The guinea pig might have eaten her already!" said Wallis and he went very pale.

"It's the most dreadful thing that's ever happened in our garden!" sniffed Stuart.

"Our garden will never be the same," whispered Wallis.

Clive tut tutted and folded several pairs of his arms. "Really," he said, "I don't know what you're fussing about. Susie's fine!"

"What?" Wallis and Stuart stared at him. Betty fluttered down from the top of the hutch. Bertie buzzed up beside Betty.

Clive waved a foot at the ground. "Look!" he said. "Susie's been here – here's her trail!"

They all looked and they could all see the silvery trail that led away from the hutch into the garden.

"SUSIE!" shouted Stuart and they rushed off to see where it went.

Along the ground went the trail, all the way to the compost heap.

Stuart, Bertie, Wallis, Betty and Clive looked all around the compost heap – but they couldn't see Susie.

"Look! There's the trail!" said Wallis and off they went again.

Along the ground went the trail, all the way to the newly planted radishes.

Stuart, Bertie, Wallis, Betty and Clive looked all around the radishes – but they couldn't see Susie.

"Look! There's the trail!" said Betty and off they went again.

Along the ground went the trail, all the way to Stuart's flower pot, where it stopped.

Stuart, Bertie, Wallis, Betty and Clive stood and looked at each other.

"Clive," said Bertie, very slowly and sadly. "That wasn't Susie's trail. It was Stuart's."

They turned and looked behind them and, sure enough, there were two silvery trails, one going away from the flower pot and the other coming back.

"Boo hoo hoo HOO!" Betty Butterfly burst into tears. "We were right all along! Susie's been eaten by a guinea pig and we'll never ever see her again! Poor poor poor Susie!"

There was a stirring at the bottom of the flower pot and a head looked out.

"Hello," said Susie Slug, with a huge yawn. "Did somebody call me?"

*"Oh," says Little Ghost. "Susie was there all the time!"*

*"That's right," says Big Ghost. "Ooooh! Time for me to have a little nap!"*

*Little Ghost nods. "I'll see you next week, Big Ghost. Thank you for the story!"*

See you next week.

# WEEK 18

*"Big Ghost! Big Ghost!" Little Ghost is floating in through the kitchen window. "Are you there?"*

*Big Ghost wakes up with a jump. He's been asleep in his favourite place on top of the cupboard.*

*"Big Ghost!" says Little Ghost. "Tell me some more about the kitten – it's ages since you told me about him!*

*"Come up here," says Big Ghost, "and I'll tell you how he got lost … "*

## The Kitten with no Name: Part Three

One day the kitten who had no name was chasing a big white butterfly. He chased it up and he chased it down and then he stopped. His mother was calling him.

"Be a good kitten," she said, "and stay right here by our hedge today. I'm going to go up to the end of the field to see what I can see and I may be a little while."

"Are you going to find our special place?" asked the kitten hopefully. "The very special place you told me about? The very special place where we can live happily for ever and ever and be hugged?"

"Not today," said his mother. "But very very soon. I'm just going to see how the weather will be tomorrow." And off she went.

The kitten watched the big white butterfly flitter out of reach and then he sat down to think.

"I'm big enough to go to the end of the field," he thought.

And then he thought, "I could give Mother a surprise! If she sees that I'm big enough to go to the end of the field, she'll see that I'm big enough to go with her to find our new home. Or maybe" – the kitten jumped up – "we could go today!"

The kitten was so excited that he began to skip up and down.

"Yes!" he said to himself. "Yes! I'll run after Mother and then she'll see what a big grown-up cat I am – and we'll find the very special place in time to go to bed!" And he scrambled away from the hedge where he and his mother had lived ever since he was born. Off he went, the way his mother had gone.

The grass in the field was long and thick. The kitten had not been there often; he usually stayed on the other side of the hedge where children played and the grass was short.

"Meeow! I can't see where to go," he said. He jumped and he bounded and he leapt …

And he leapt and he bounded and he jumped.

And he bounded and he leapt and he jumped.

And he bounded.

And he stopped.

"I'm tired," said the kitten and he was. His paws hurt and there was grass seed in his fur.

"I think I'll go home," said the kitten.

He turned himself round and round and then round again.

"Which way is home?" he thought. "Is it this way?"

But it wasn't.

"Is it that way?" he wondered.

But it wasn't.

"It must be this way," said the kitten.

But it wasn't.

"Oh dear," said the kitten and he sat down under a large thistle. "I think I'm lost." Two big tears rolled down his nose.

Poor kitten. He's lost.

93

There was a rustling in the grass and a squeaking.

The kitten sniffed loudly. "Mother?" he said hopefully.

A mouse popped her head out from under a thistle leaf. "Oh my whistling whiskers!" she said. "It's a kitten!"

The kitten sniffed again. "Hello," he said. "Have you seen my mother?"

"No," said the mouse. She looked nervously over her shoulder. "Is she near?"

"I don't know," said the kitten. "I'm lost."

"Oh." The mouse sat down beside him. "Where do you live?"

"Under a big green hedge," said the kitten. "But I don't know which way to go."

"A big hedge?" said the mouse. "That's easy. You see that yellow gorse bush over there?"

The kitten looked. "Yes," he said.

"The big hedge is just a step and a hop further on," said the mouse and she twitched her tail and skipped away.

"Thank you!" said the kitten and he began jumping …

and bounding …

and leaping …

all the way to the yellow gorse bush.

When he got there he stopped. Yes! There in front of him was a big hedge.

"Hurrah!" said the kitten. "I'll soon be home now." He yawned. "But I'm very tired. Maybe I'll have a little sleep and then I'll run home. Mother won't be home just yet."

He crept under the shelter of the gorse bush and curled himself up into a neat little ball.

"Purr," he said to himself. "This is a very pretty bush. I wonder why I didn't see it before?"

And he closed his eyes and began to dream of a very special place covered in pretty yellow flowers … a warm and cosy place to live in for ever and ever.

Turn to page 126 for the next kitten story.

*Little Ghost sighs happily. "I do like hearing about the kitten," he says. "But I want to hear some more about the children too!"*

*"Next week," says Big Ghost.*

*"Couldn't you tell me just a TINY story now?" begs Little Ghost.*

*"Not even the tiniest story," says Big Ghost. "See you next week, Little Ghost!"*

# WEEK 19

*There's a wind blowing and Little Ghost is blown twice round the chimney pots before he can fly down to the front door of the house.*

*"OoooooooooH!" Little Ghost pops through the keyhole and into the hall.*
*"Hello, Big Ghost! I'm here!"*

*Big Ghost is sitting comfortably on top of a pile of coats.*
*"Tonight I'm going to tell you a story about Jason," he says.*

## Jason's New Shoes

It was a Tuesday morning when Mum noticed that Jason's shoes were pinching his toes.

"We'll go and have a look in the market," Mum said.

"Can I have blue trainers?" Jason asked.

"We'll see what we can find," Mum said.

They were just about to go out through the garden gate when Granny Annie came hurrying towards them.

"Where are you off to?" she asked.

"We're going to the market," said Jason.
"We're going to buy blue trainers for me."

"That's nice," said Granny Annie. "I was thinking of going to the market myself. I'd like to buy myself a bright red jumper. Can I come with you?"

"Of course you can," said Jason.

Jason and Mum and Granny Annie went down the road. They hadn't gone far when there was a hurry and a flurry and Ross came rushing up behind them.

"Wait for me!" he said. "I want to come to the market too! Julius says they've got supersonic, extra-special, high-flying kites at the toy stall. I want to get one."

"I'm going to have new blue trainers," said Jason. He looked thoughtfully at Ross. "If you come with us I could help you choose your kite. You could have a blue one to match my trainers. And I could help you fly it on the way home."

"A bright red kite would be fun," said Granny Annie. "And it would match my bright red jumper."

"Or a yellow one," said Mum. "A yellow one to match the bananas."

"What bananas?" asked Jason.

"The bananas I'm going to buy at the market," said Mum.

"We need oranges too," said Ross.

"OK," said Mum. "I'll get oranges as well."

Jason, Mum, Granny Annie and Ross arrived at the market.

"Fruit stall first," said Mum and she bought bananas and oranges and pears and apples and grapes and a melon.

"Let's go and look at the jumpers," said Granny Annie. She led them round the corner to the wool shop and she bought a bright red jumper with a matching bobble hat.

"I want to get my kite now," said Ross and they walked along to the toys.

"Wow!" said Jason. "Look at all the different colours!"

"Hello!" said a voice and there was Julius with Daisy B and the twins, Tia and Tim. They were looking at the toys too. Daisy B was carrying a little pink basket.

"Look!" said Daisy B. "Look what Daisy B got! It's a pink basket! It's a basket for my kitty."

"Fat Freda's much too big to fit in there," said Tia. "You need a proper basket."

Daisy B shook her head. "It's a little basket for my little kitty."

Julius sighed. "She keeps talking about this little kitty," he said. "I think it must be a pretend one. She's spent all her pocket money on that basket."

"I think she's talking about the kitten we saw in the field when we were going to the swings," Ross said.

Daisy B nodded her head. "Kitty coming soon," she said. "Daisy B's kitty."

"It was a very pretty kitty," said Tia. "Wasn't it, Jason?"

There was no answer.

Everyone looked round.

Jason wasn't there.

"Quick!" said Mum. "Everybody look for him!"

Mum, Granny Annie, Ross, Julius, Daisy B and Tia and Tim ran to see if Jason was still looking at the fruit.

He wasn't there.

They rushed round the corner to the wool shop.

He wasn't there.

They hurried to the market café in case he'd felt hungry.

He wasn't there.

"Oh! I know where he is!" said Ross and he dashed off towards the shoe stall.

Mum, Granny Annie, Julius, Daisy B and Tia and Tim dashed after him –

and there was Jason.

"Hello," he said. "I got bored waiting to buy my trainers. Look! They've got blue ones!"

"Jason!" said Mum as she gave him a huge hug. "You must NEVER go off on your own! I was worried we'd lost you!"

"Sorry," said Jason. "Can we buy my trainers now?"

"I don't know if you deserve new shoes," Mum said, but she was smiling.

"PLEASE!" said Jason. "I promise I'll never go off on my own again – and my other shoes pinch my toes. You said so!"

Mum laughed. "All right, Jason – you can have your trainers."

They bought Jason's new blue trainers and then everyone went to the café for a cup of tea.

"I'm worn out," said Mum. "Still, at least we've got everything."

"No we haven't," said Ross. "I haven't got my kite!"

"Oh, Ross!" said Mum. "I can't go back to the toy stall again!"

"It's OK," Ross said. "I can go on my own."

"Can I come with you?" Jason asked.

"No," said Ross. "You stay here."

"But I want you to buy a blue one to match my trainers," Jason said.

"Or a red one to match my jumper," said Granny Annie.

"Pink one," said Daisy B.

"Yellow," said Mum.

Tia and Tim grabbed the bag of oranges out of Mum's basket. "Orange!" they shouted.

Julius threw the melon in the air and caught it. "What about green?" he said.

"It's my pocket money," Ross said and he zoomed off.

Five minutes later he was back with a big brown parcel. "Here we are!" he said.

"Can we fly it on the way home?" asked Jason.

"Ross can fly it in the garden," said Mum.

And that's just what Ross did and it wasn't a blue or a red or a pink or a yellow or an orange or a green kite. It was black with silver stars. But it did have a rainbow-coloured tail that whirled and twirled as it flew high above Jason's head as he ran and he jumped in his new blue trainers.

*Little Ghost is sitting up very straight and looking most excited. "Big Ghost! Big Ghost! I know what Daisy B was talking about! The kitten she saw by the swings was the kitten with no name – the kitten that you tell me stories about!"*

*Big Ghost nods. "That's right, Little Ghost."*

*"Do you think his name is Pretty Kitty?" Little Ghost asks.*

*Big Ghost laughs. "You'll have to wait and see, Little Ghost. Now – off you go!"*

*Little Ghost squeezes through the keyhole and blows away home on the wind.*

# WEEK 20

Big Ghost isn't in the hall of the big old house. He isn't in the kitchen. He isn't on the stairs.

"Ooooooh!" calls Little Ghost. "Where are yooooooooou?"

"Here!" Big Ghost pops his head out of a doorway.

"OH!" says little Ghost. "I forgot about the playroom!" He looks at all the different toys scattered over the floor. "Can we have a story about animals?"

"See if you can guess what this is!" says Big Ghost.

## Splash!

From a spot
To a comma.
From a comma
To a wriggle.
From a wriggle
In an egg
A squishy jelly egg
To a wriggle in the water
Swimming here, swimming there …

Tadpole!

Growing big

Growing bigger

Swimming here

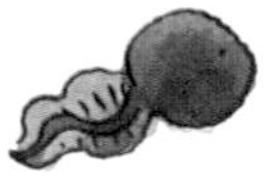

Swimming there

Little legs

At the back

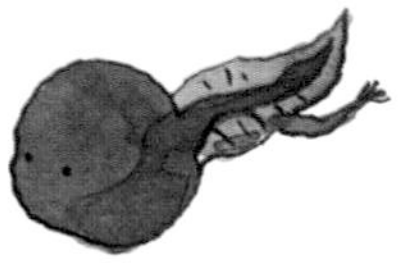

Growing long

Growing strong.

Little legs

At the front

Growing long

Growing strong

And a mouth

That is wide

And a hop

Hop hop hop –

Splish!

Frog!

Splash!

"I KNEW it was a frog!" says Little Ghost. "Please can you tell me about some more animals next time?"

"All right, I'll meet you here next week," says Big Ghost. "Don't forget!"

"I won't," says Little Ghost and he waves goodbye to the farm animals and the Noah's Ark animals and the teddies and the dolls and the little clockwork train.

"Little Ghost," says Big Ghost, "if you wave goodbye to every single one of the toys, you'll be very late home."

Little Ghost giggles. "All right," he says. "Bye!" And he floats away up the chimney.

# WEEK 21

*Little Ghost is already waiting in the playroom when Big Ghost floats up through the ceiling from the kitchen.*

*"Hello," he says. "I'm ready for my story!"*

*Big Ghost looks at the Noah's Ark. All the animals are tucked inside tonight – except one.*

*"I'll tell you about Monkey," he says.*

*"Good!" says Little Ghost and he settles down to listen.*

 **Snap!**

It was very early in the morning, but Monkey was wide awake. He hopped out of bed and grabbed a banana.

"I'm going fishing today!" he sang and he tossed the banana skin into a bush.

"I'm going fishing today!"

Monkey went swinging through the trees. He was going to meet his good friend Bearcub and they were going to spend the day fishing in the river.

"I'm going fishing today!" sang Monkey as he swung through the trees.

"I'm going fishing today!"

Bearcub was waiting for Monkey on the river bank. He had two fishing rods and a bucket of worms.

"Are you ready, Monkey?" he asked.

"I certainly am!" said Monkey and they sat down together to fish.

They fished for five minutes … and they caught nothing at all.

They fished for ten minutes … and they caught nothing at all.

They fished for fifteen minutes … and they caught nothing at all.

"H'm," said Monkey. "Where have all the fish gone?"

"I don't know," said Bearcub. "Shall I jump in the water and look?"

"All right," said Monkey and Bearcub held his nose and jumped into the water.

"Ooof!" he said as he bobbed up again. "It's very cold."

"Can you see any fish?" asked Monkey.

"No," said Bearcub. "All I can see is green wavy weed and a long brown log."

Monkey rubbed his nose. "Maybe if we stood on the long brown log we'd catch more fish?"

"That's a good idea," said Bearcub. "I'll go and get it."

He splashed back into the river and began to wade towards the long brown log –

and the long brown log opened a huge toothy mouth –

and **SNAP!** Bearcub was caught by his little stumpy tail.

"Help!" he shouted. "Help! Help! Help!"

"Be quiet," said the crocodile and he kept his teeth shut tight as he talked. "It's no good shouting. I'm going to cook you and eat you for my tea."

Monkey was watching from the bank.

He saw Crocodile catch his good friend Bearcub.

"H'm," he said to himself. "Crocodiles are clever – but monkeys are cleverer!"

"Hey! Crocodile!" he called.

Crocodile looked up at Monkey. "What do you want?"

Oh no! What can Bearcub do now?

he asked and he kept his teeth shut tight on Bearcub's little stumpy tail.

"Oh, nothing much," said Monkey. "I just wondered if you knew how to make the very best ever Bearcub stew. My old great-granny told me, but I bet she didn't tell you."

"What sort of stew is that?" asked Crocodile and he kept his teeth shut tight on Bearcub's little stumpy tail.

"It's the most mouthwatering, delicious, fantastical stew ever," said Monkey. "But you have to have a pineapple."

"A pineapple?" said Crocodile and he still kept his teeth shut tight on Bearcub's little stumpy tail. "Where would I get a pineapple?"

"I'll fetch you one," said Monkey and he swung away into the jungle. He was back in two minutes with a big, beautiful, yellow pineapple and he put it carefully down on the edge of the river bank.

Crocodile's eyes gleamed. "Give it to me," he said and he kept his teeth shut tight as tight on Bearcub's little stumpy tail.

"Oh no," said Monkey. "For my old great-granny's Bearcub stew you need mangoes as well."

"Mangoes?" said Crocodile and he kept his teeth shut tight tight tight on Bearcub's little stumpy tail. "Where would I get mangoes?"

"I'll fetch you some," said Monkey, and he

swung away into the jungle. He was back in three minutes with four soft, sweet, squashy mangoes and he put them down carefully on the edge of the river bank.

Crocodile's eyes shone. "Give them to me," he said, still keeping his teeth tight shut on Bearcub's little stumpy tail.

"Oh no," said Monkey. "For my old great-granny's Bearcub stew you need coconuts as well."

"Coconuts?" said Crocodile and all the while his teeth stayed shut tight on Bearcub's stumpy little tail. "Where would I get coconuts?"

"I'll fetch you some," said Monkey and he swung away into the jungle. He was back in five minutes with six hard hairy coconuts full of crisp white flesh and he put them down carefully on the edge of the river bank.

Crocodile's eyes sparkled. "Give them to me," he said and his teeth never once let go of Bearcub's stumpy little tail.

"No," said Monkey. "I've fetched you all the things you need to make the most mouthwatering, delicious, fantastical stew ever and you haven't ever said please. Or thank you. I think I'll eat them all myself." And he bent down to pick up an armful of coconuts.

"PLEASE!" roared the crocodile and his mouth opened wide. "PLEASE!"

"Here you are, then," said Monkey and he threw the coconuts just as hard as ever he could and they plopped neatly into Crocodile's wide open mouth.

"Hup! Hup! Hup!" hiccupped Crocodile.

"Ho ho ho!" laughed Monkey.

"Thank you, Monkey," said Bearcub as he pulled himself out of the river and safely on to the river bank.

Then Monkey and Bearcub took the pineapple and the mangoes and went off to have a picnic, but they left the rest of the coconuts for Crocodile, just in case he ever wanted to make Monkey's old great-granny's coconut crumble.

*"Do Tia and Tim like playing with their animals?" asks Little Ghost.*

*"I think they like lots of different games," says Big Ghost. Little Ghost looks hopeful. "Will you –"*

*"Next week," says Big Ghost, interrupting him. "I'll tell you a story about Tia and Tim next week."*

*"See you then," says Little Ghost and he whisks off up the chimney.*

# WEEK 22

*Big Ghost is in the kitchen this week, fast asleep under the sink. Little Ghost wakes him up.*

*"It's time for my story," he says. "You said you were going to tell me some more about Tia and Tim!"*

*"I'll tell you about the time when they were cross," says Big Ghost and he and Little Ghost sit down together on the draining board.*

## When Tia and Tim were Cross

It all began with the parcel from Visiting Dad. He sent the parcel to Tia and Tim and when they opened it they found a game of Snakes and Ladders and a jigsaw puzzle.

"I'll have the Snakes and Ladders," Tim said quickly. "You can have the jigsaw puzzle, Tia."

"I don't want it!" Tia said. "I want the Snakes and Ladders!"

"Too bad," said Tim and he ran up to his room and hid the box under his bed.

Tia waited until Tim was out playing football with Ross and then she tiptoed into Tim's room and took the box away.

She left the jigsaw puzzle there instead.

When Tim found out he was very angry, but Tia wouldn't tell him where she had hidden the Snakes and Ladders.

"They're mine!" she said and although Tim searched her room and threw her duvet and pillow on the floor, he couldn't find the box anywhere.

Tia and Tim went on being cross with each other. Tia's friends came to tea and they tried to play rounders in the garden, but Tim kept getting in the way.

"Butterfingers!" he yelled when Cathy missed an easy catch.

"Look!" And he picked the ball up and threw it high in the air and then caught it with one hand.

"Show off!" said Tia.

"Hey!" Tim said when Claudia dropped the ball. "I'll throw that for you!" And he threw the ball so hard that it landed in the roses and Tia got scratched when she went to fetch it.

"Tim," Tia said. "Go away!"

When Tia was running to score a rounder Tim stuck out his foot and tripped her up.

"You're mean!" Tia said. "I'm going to tell Mum!" And she threw the ball at Tim as hard as she could.

Aren't they being naughty!

Tim ducked … and there was a loud **CRASH!**

Tia, Cathy, Claudia, Kim, Emmie and Tim froze.

"That's Mum's greenhouse!" Tia said in a horrified voice. "She'll be furious!"

Mum was.

Cathy, Claudia, Kim and Emmie were sent home early and Tia was sent upstairs to her bedroom. All the way up the stairs she shouted, "It was Tim's fault! It was Tim's fault!" But nobody wanted to listen to her.

Tia slammed the bedroom door and sat on her bed in a terrible rage. "I'll get my own back," she said. "Just you wait, horrible bossyboots beastly Tim!"

Two days later Tim's friend Winston came to tea. He and Tim went out to ride their bikes up and down the garden path and Tia went too.

When Tim tried to do a wheelie and fell off Tia laughed, very loudly.

"It's not funny, Tia," said Tim.

When Winston was trying to do a brake spin Tia dropped her skipping rope on the path and Winston skidded into the hollyhocks.

"Go away, Tia," shouted Tim.

Tim and Winston decided to have a race and Tia called Hunter just as they shouted one two three GO! and Hunter came barking and yapping down the path and they had to stop.

"Tia," yelled Tim, "you're horrible!" And he picked up Tia's skipping rope

and threw it in the pond. Hunter dashed after it and came out wet and dripping and knocked over the post that held up the washing line just as Mum came hurrying up the garden path to see what was going on.

Everyone talked at once. Tim said it was Tia's fault. Tia said it was Tim's fault because Tim had made her break the glass in the greenhouse. Tim said he'd never have got Tia into trouble if she hadn't taken his Snakes and Ladders. Tia said it wasn't his, it was hers. Winston said he was sorry about the hollyhocks. Hunter barked and jumped and put his dirty wet paws all over the clean washing and then dragged the skipping rope across the path and Mum stepped backwards, caught her foot and sat down with a bump!

Tia and Tim and Winston stood still in horrified silence … and then Mum began to laugh. Tia and Tim looked at each other and then they began to laugh too. Winston began to giggle and Hunter bounded round and round in a circle.

"You know what we should all do," said Mum when she had stopped laughing. "First of all we should pick up the dirty washing and then we should play a game. Something without bats and balls and dogs and bikes. Something quiet. An indoor kind of game." She looked at Tia and winked in a meaningful sort of way. "I don't suppose you can think of a game that would be fun for four people to play?" She winked again. "A game that's no fun at all for only one person?"

"Oh," said Tia. "Well … yes." And she ran indoors ahead of Mum and the boys and as they sat down in the kitchen, she put the box of Snakes and Ladders on the table.

"Who's going to begin?" Mum asked.

Tia looked at Tim. "You can," she said.

Tim looked at Tia. "No – you can."

"I think," said Mum, "we'll let Winston begin."

And as Winston began to rattle the dice Tim pushed at Tia's foot under the table. "Sorry," he said, very softly.

"Me too," said Tia.

"After we've played this," Tim said, "can we all do the jigsaw puzzle?"

*Little Ghost nods. "I like Tia and Tim.
And Tia's friends – those girls – they were the children who
came to her birthday party, weren't they?"*

*"That's right," says Big Ghost.*

*"So will you tell me another story about them next week?" says Little Ghost.*

*"I was thinking I might tell you about the rabbits," says Big Ghost.*

*"Ooooh YES!" says Little Ghost. "I'll meet you by the rabbit hutches!"*

# WEEK 23

*It's not a very warm night, but Big Ghost is snoozing happily in the spare straw by Fluffy's hutch.*

*"This is nice," says Little Ghost as he snuggles in too. "I'm all ready for my rabbit story. Are you awake, Big Ghost?"*

*"Yes," says Big Ghost. "I am now. Shall we begin?"*

## Millie and Tillie

One day Mrs Rabbit decided to take her two little rabbits on a picnic.

"We will have lettuce sandwiches," she said, "and parsnip cake. And carrot biscuits."

Millie and Tillie Rabbit rubbed their tummies.

"Goodie goodie goodie!" they said.

"And I shall take my deck chair and a cushion," said Mrs Rabbit. "I like to be comfortable on a picnic."

"Can we take our kites?" asked Millie.

"Of course, my little bunnikins," said Mrs Rabbit. "Now, I wonder if I should take a rug? It might get cold."

"And I want to take my bicycle," said Tillie.

"And I want to take my scooter," said Millie.

"What a good idea, my little fluffy tails," said Mrs Rabbit. "Father Rabbit, do you think I should take a hot water bottle?"

Father Rabbit looked up from reading the paper. "It might be a good idea," he said. "You always say it's a good thing to be ready for anything."

"Are you coming too, Father?" asked Tillie. "We can play races!"

Father Rabbit yawned. "Maybe another time," he said.

"Do come too," said Millie. "You can fly my kite!"

"I'm tired today," said Father Rabbit. "You can tell me all about it when you get home."

"PLEASE come," said Tillie. "You can watch me ride my bicycle!"

"Yes," said Millie. "And we can all play hide and seek!"

Father Rabbit shook his head. "I'm rather busy just now," he said. "I'm going to read my paper."

"I think I will take the hot water bottle," said Mrs Rabbit. "And we'd better take umbrellas too. And be sure to bring your coats and sun hats, my little pretties. Now, I wonder if I should take the kettle? We'll need to fill it with water, of course. And perhaps a little table …"

Mrs Rabbit, Millie and Tillie set out across the fields. There were so many things to carry, they had to go very slowly.

"I don't think we'll go too far, my little darlings," said Mrs Rabbit. "I think we'll have our picnic under the tall pine tree."

"Good idea!" puffed Millie.

"Yes!" panted Tillie.

When they reached the tree they put everything down. Mrs Rabbit put up her deck chair. Millie and Tillie spread out the rug. They piled up the umbrellas and the sun hats and the coats and plumped up Mrs Rabbit's cushion.

"Time for a lovely cup of tea, my precious poppets," said Mrs Rabbit. "Run and find some firewood."

"Look!" said Tillie. "There's an old newspaper in my bicycle basket! Can't we use that for the fire?"

"We'll need sticks as well," said Millie.

The two little rabbits ran here and there picking up sticks. They piled them up neatly on the scrumpled newspaper and Mrs Rabbit lit the fire. They balanced the kettle on the top and it began to hiss and bubble almost at once.

"There!" said Mrs Rabbit. "Isn't this fun? Now all we have to do is put out the picnic things."

"Hurrah!" said Millie.

There was a pause.

"Mother," said Millie, "where's the picnic basket?"

"Tillie was carrying it, my little sweetie pie," said Mrs Rabbit.

"I wasn't," said Tillie. "I thought Millie was carrying it."

"I was carrying the rug and the umbrellas and the sunhats and the hot water bottle and the kettle," Millie said.

They all looked at each other. Then Mrs Rabbit peered hopefully under the deck chair.

There was no picnic basket there.

Tillie rushed to look under the coats.

There was no picnic basket there either.

Millie dashed to look under the rug. There was no sign of any picnic basket.

Mrs Rabbit sat down in her deck chair with a little sigh. "Oh dearie me," she said. "It won't be much of a picnic if we haven't got anything to eat."

"And I'm very hungry!" said Millie.

"Me too!" said Tillie.

"Should we go home again and fetch it?" asked Millie.

"I'm too tired," said Tillie and she flopped down on the rug. Millie sat down beside her and the kettle began to sing a bubbly little song.

Mrs Rabbit's eyes closed.

Tillie and Millie snuggled up together and fell fast asleep. The kettle went on softly bubbling.

"Wake up! It's picnic time!" said a loud voice.

Mrs Rabbit opened her eyes. Tillie and Millie sat up with a jump.

There were the lettuce sandwiches. There was the parsnip cake. There were the carrot biscuits, all neatly laid out on the rug … and there was Father Rabbit busily making tea.

"Father!" shouted Tillie and Millie.

Father Rabbit smiled. "It was very odd," he said. "After you'd gone I couldn't find my newspaper anywhere. I looked high and low – and then I saw your picnic basket. It was on the doorstep, so I thought perhaps I'd bring it out to you. And here I am!"

"That's lovely!" said Mother Rabbit.

Tillie and Millie looked at each other and then at the fire. There was no sign of the newspaper, only a few black ashes.

"Father," said Tillie, "I think we made a mistake."

"Yes," said Millie. "We really didn't mean to –"

"It was in my bicycle basket," said Tillie.

"And we used it for the fire," said Millie.

"We're very sorry," they said together.

Father Rabbit looked at them in surprise. "What are you talking about?" he asked.

"Your paper," said Millie.

"We burnt it all up," said Tillie.

Father Rabbit began to laugh. "No no no," he said and he pulled a newspaper from inside his jacket. "You must have found an old one. I found mine under the basket. I'll read it after our picnic."

"Oh!" said Tillie.

"Hurrah!" said Millie.

"What funny little bunnies you are!" said Mrs Rabbit fondly.

"Yes," said Father Rabbit. "And now it's time for lettuce sandwiches!"

And they ate every last crumb of the sandwiches and the parsnip cake and the carrot biscuits … and afterwards Father Rabbit didn't read his paper. He watched Tillie ride her bike … and Millie ride her scooter … and he flew a kite … and Millie and Tillie ran races … and after that they all played hide and seek.

"Oooh," said Tillie. "This is the best picnic ever."

And it was.

*Little Ghost is very quiet as Big Ghost finishes the story.*

*"Little Ghost?" says Big Ghost. "Are you asleep?"*

*Little Ghost sits up at once. "No," he says. He looks up at the hutch. "Did you enjoy that story, Fluffy Rabbit?"*

*Fluffy doesn't answer. She's too busy nibbling at a carrot.*

*Little Ghost yawns a huge yawn. "Oooooh!"*

*"Little Ghost," says Big Ghost, "I think it's time you went home!"*

*And Little Ghost yawns again as he floats away …*

# WEEK 24

*"Big Ghost! Big Ghost!" Little Ghost is flying down the hall. "Big Ghost! I've seen the kitten who doesn't have a name! He was sitting on the doorstep washing his paws when I came in … PLEASE will you tell me some more about him?"*

*Big Ghost wanders out of the kitchen.*

*"Sit down on the stairs, Little Ghost," he says, "and I'll tell you how the kitten met a frog … "*

## The Kitten with no Name: Part Four

The kitten who had no name slept and slept. When he woke up it was getting late.

"Meeow!" said the kitten. He stood up and stretched. "I must hurry home. Mother's sure to be back by now. Which way is my hedge?"

He looked about and there, sure enough, was a big green hedge. It wasn't far away at all.

"I'd better hurry," said the kitten. He ran with a hop and a skip and a jump and he didn't look where he was going.

*SPLASH!*

The kitten fell into a stream.

The water was very very cold … and the kitten couldn't swim.

"Meeeeow!" he shrieked. "Meeeeow! Mother! Mother! Meeeeow!"

Down and down he sank and then up and up he bobbed again. Down and down …

"Flip my flippers," said a croaky voice.

Someone or something seized the kitten by the scruff of the neck. Someone or something pulled him out of the stream.

"Flip my flippers and what have we got here?"

The kitten opened his eyes. A large green frog was standing in front of him.

"You should learn to swim, young animal," said the frog. "You could drown yourself jumping in like that."

He began to rub the kitten's wet fur with a handful of grass.

"Not that it wasn't a good jump. Not as good as us frogs do, of course, but not bad. Not bad at all." He picked another handful of grass.

The kitten gave a feeble mew. The frog was steadily rubbing him dry again, but he still felt cold.

The frog suddenly stopped. "Dear me! Are you meant to be furry?" he asked.

The kitten nodded.

"That's all right, then." The frog went on rubbing. "I wondered if the water had done something funny to your scales. Or your feathers." He gave the kitten a final pat. "Go on, then. Tell us what you are."

"I'm a kitten," said the kitten. "I was trying to get home, but the stream got in the way." And he began to cry.

"Now now now," said the frog. "We don't need tears. Tears never sorted anything. What we need is action!"

"Do we?" asked the kitten.

The frog nodded. "I'll get you sorted out – no trouble. You just curl up here by the dandelions and have a little snooze. I'll go and get my friend. He'll take you over the stream – no trouble."

The kitten yawned. He did feel tired and the evening sun was beginning to feel warm and comfortable on his back.

"Thank you very much," he said and he curled himself up by the dandelions. "Will your friend really help me?"

"Sure as tadpoles turn into frogs," said the frog. He hopped away – and then jumped back.

"Hey – no more swimming. Right?"

"Right," said the sleepy kitten.

"Good," said the frog and he jumped into the stream with a plop!

The kitten yawned again. "I'll soon be back with my mother," he thought. "We'll soon be together again … and then we can find our very special place … all warm and cosy … and someone there will love us and hug us … " and he drifted off to sleep.

*"Frogs do come from tadpoles," says Little Ghost. "You told me a story about them, didn't you?"*

*"That's right," says Big Ghost.*

*Little Ghost gets up very slowly. "I wish I knew what happened to the kitten when the frog came back," he says.*

*"You'll find out soon," says Big Ghost.*

*"When?" asks Little Ghost.*

*"Wait and see," says Big Ghost.*

# WEEK 25

*"OooooooooooH!" Little Ghost rushes into the kitchen. "Big Ghost! I'm late! I was playing with the spider in the water-spout outside and I got stuck! My mama says I can only have a VERY little story … I nearly couldn't come at all!"*

*Big Ghost floats over from his cupboard. "Never mind, Little Ghost," he says. "You're here now – and I've just the right story for you!"*

## Up the Water-spout

Look! There's a spout
   With water dripping out.
   Where does it go to?
   Where does it go?
   Oh.
   It goes up …
   And up and up …
   Where does it go?
   Let's see!
   Up I go
   Up and up

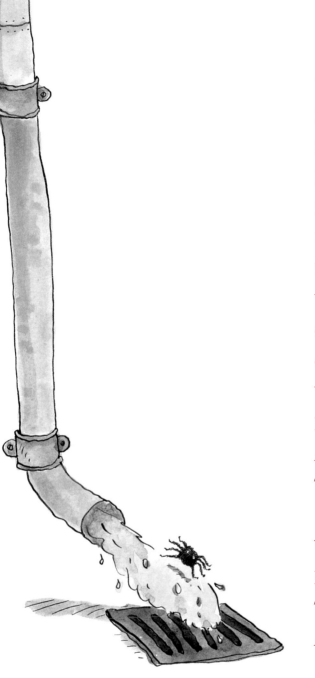

Up and up …

Phew!

Stop and puff.

Here I go again

Here I go

Up and up

Up and up …

WHOOOOOOSH!

Oh oh oh

Oh oh OH!

Whoosh comes the water

Down I go …

All the way down

To the ground.

What a lot of rain!

I think I'll sit in the sun

Then I think I'll climb the spout

Again.

"I'll tell that story to the spider next time I see him!" says Little Ghost.

"You do that," says Big Ghost. "And now you'd better hurry home. I can hear Mama Ghost calling you … "

*Big Ghost is in the playroom when Little Ghost arrives. Little Ghost is just about to sit down on a box when he stops to listen.*

*"Big Ghost!" he says. "What's that noise?"*

*"It's Julius singing to Dasiy B," says Big Ghost. "She fell over today and she hurt her knee and now she can't get to sleep."*

*"Poor Daisy B," says Little Ghost. He picks up a bear from the floor. "Do you know a falling over story, Big Ghost?"*

*"I know JUST the right story!" says Big Ghost.*

## When Little Bear Cried and Cried

Little Bear was dancing. First he was a bird, soaring high. Then he was an aeroplane, roaring through the clouds. Then he was a whirligig, whirling and twirling. Round and round and round he danced, round and round and round until –

*Crash!*

Little Bear fell over.

"Ooooh! Ooooh! Ooooh!" Little Bear cried and cried.

Buddy Bear came running to see what the noise was.

Poor Little Bear.

"Ooooh! Ooooh! Ooooh!" Little Bear cried louder.

"Don't be a baby, Little Bear," said Buddy. "Be brave! I'm always brave when I hurt myself!"

But Little Bear didn't want to be brave. He wanted someone to be sorry for him and to kiss him better.

"Ooooh! Ooooh! Ooooh!" he wailed.

"Hey hey, young Bear!" said Old Bear. "What's all the crying about? Why don't we find you a drink and a biscuit?"

But Little Bear didn't want a drink and a biscuit. He wanted someone to hug him tightly and be sorry for him and to kiss him better. He cried even louder. "Ooooh! Ooooh! Ooooh!"

Big Bear came out to see what was going on.

"Little Bear! Little Bear!" she called. "Come inside!"

But Little Bear didn't want to go inside. He wanted someone to come and find him and to hug him tightly and be sorry for him and to kiss him better.

"Ooooh! Ooooh! Ooooh!" he cried. "Ooooh! Ooooh! Ooooh!"

Someone came hurrying along the path. Someone found Little Bear and hugged him very tightly.

Someone said, "Poor Little Bear! Poor, poor Little Bear" – and someone kissed him better over and over again.

Little Bear stopped crying.

"I fell over, Daddy Bear," he said. "I was dancing and I fell over and no one came."

Daddy Bear gave him another kiss. "I know, Little Bear. It was terrible."

Little Bear jumped up. "I'm all better now," he said. "Look, Daddy Bear, look! Watch me dancing!"

Daddy Bear nodded. "Very good, Little Bear!"

"Dance with me, Daddy Bear!" said Little Bear. "Let's dance together!"

And Little Bear and Daddy Bear danced. First they were birds whirling high. Then they were aeroplanes roaring through the clouds. Then they were whirligigs whirling and twirling. Round and round and round they danced until they were dizzy and they fell over in a heap

Crash!

And they laughed and laughed and laughed.

*"I can't hear any more singing," says Little Ghost. "Do you think Daisy B is asleep now?"*

*"I expect so," says Big Ghost.*

*"She'd like that story," says Little Ghost and he gets up to go. "Was she dancing when she fell over?"*

*"I think she was," says Big Ghost.*

*"I'm going to dance all the way home," Little Ghost tells him. "Goodbye!"*

# WEEK 27

*A pigeon is cooing in the garden as Little Ghost slides in through the kitchen window for his story.*

*"Big Ghost," Little Ghost says, "those birds always make that noise. But why do they do it?"*

*"I'll tell you the story that a pigeon once told me," says Big Ghost. "But it's a long story, so make yourself comfortable."*

Coo! Coo! Coo!

In the beginning of time Mighty Pigeon made the world. He made sky to fly in. He made earth to scratch in. He made trees to roost in and he made a big blue lake full of water for drinking. Then he chose the very finest grey and white cloud and pulled it down from the sky. He cut it up to make hundreds and hundreds of brand new pigeons and tossed them into the brand new world.

After that Mighty Pigeon had a little rest and a little scratch.

The brand new pigeons liked their brand new world. They flew in the sky and scratched in the earth.

They roosted in the trees and they drank the water from the lake … and then they rested and had a little scratch, just like Mighty Pigeon.

Mighty Pigeon watched them proudly. "Isn't life good?" he asked them. "Isn't it good to be alive?"

"It certainly is," said the biggest brand new pigeon, "but when do we get our dinner?"

"Dinner?" said Mighty Pigeon. "Why, you scratch in the earth for beetles and bugs. You look among the leaves of the trees for seeds and fruit."

The biggest brand new pigeon sniffed. "Sounds like hard work," he said. "Can't you magic up something a bit easier?"

Mighty Pigeon shook his head. "Hard work will keep you happy," he said.

The biggest brand new pigeon made a very rude noise. "Pooh to that," he said. "We're quite happy without hard work. Hard work makes a pigeon tired. Besides, it'll spoil our feathers. Pooh to hard work, that's what we say – pooh! Pooh! Pooh!" And all the brand new pigeons began to strut about shouting, "Pooh! Pooh! Pooh!"

Mighty Pigeon was angry. Mighty Pigeon was very angry. Mighty Pigeon's eyes flashed and his beak snapped. "Very well," he said, "I'll make people. They'll have two legs and no wings and they'll grow corn and crops and little green plants for you to eat. They'll build houses where you can roost. They'll fill the world with their rubbish and litter and what is rubbish and litter to them will be food and drink for you. But it won't all be easy. There'll be a problem –"

"Stop right there," said the biggest brand new pigeon. "That sounds just fine to me. What do the rest of you think?"

The other brand new pigeons jumped up and down in excitement. "Yes! Yes! Yes!"

"The answer's yes," said the biggest brand new pigeon. "Get busy, Mighty Pigeon – we'd like those people as soon as possible."

Mighty Pigeon flapped his wings. Mighty Pigeon flew round and round and round in a circle and the wind stirred up the mud at the bottom of the lake and men and women and children came hurrying out … and they were followed by cats and rats and dogs and hundreds of other animals.

The humans did all the things that Mighty Pigeon had promised. They grew corn and crops and little green plants – but when the not quite so new pigeons came hurrying down to eat, the men and women shouted and yelled and chased them away. They built houses – but when the not quite so new pigeons roosted on the roofs they found the chimneys puffed out hot black smoke. The rubbish and litter were full of good things to eat, but there were cats and rats and dogs rummaging about as well – and the not so new pigeons were not happy at all.

The biggest not so new pigeon went to see Mighty Pigeon.

"Look here, Mighty Pigeon," he said. "You've cheated us. We want you to get rid of those humans." They're a nuisance. We want to go back to the way things were."

Mighty Pigeon shook his head. "It's too late," he said. "You wanted people – now you've got them. Anyway, some of them have turned out quite nicely. Much better than I expected, actually. Have a look around."

The biggest not so new pigeon stamped his foot. "You're not listening," he said. "We don't like people! We say pooh to them! Pooh! Pooh! Pooh!"

"Pooh! Pooh! Pooh!" shouted all the other not so new pigeons.

Mighty Pigeon stood up. Mighty Pigeon took a deep breath and his feathers fluffed and puffed and puffed and fluffed until he was as big as a mountain.

"Enough is enough!" he said. "I'm FED UP with your moaning and groaning. You wouldn't listen when I tried to tell you about the humans – so now you'll just have to put up with them. And I'm FED UP with you shouting pooh! Pooh! Pooh! You're a horrible ungrateful lot and I wish I'd never made you – but I have, so it's too late. All I've got to say now is POOH! to all of YOU – and I'm going to live on the top of that very tall mountain over there for ever and ever and ever. Goodbye!"

And Mighty Pigeon flew away and the not so new pigeons never saw him again.

"Huh!" said the biggest not so new pigeon. "Well! What a way to behave!"

And he tried to say, "Pooh!" … but he couldn't. All he could say was, "COO!" … and all pigeons have been saying coo! Coo! Coo! ever since …

*Little Ghost is giggling. "Pooh," he says, "pooh! I'll know what to say next time I see the pigeons outside!"*

   *"Maybe you should feel sorry for them," says Big Ghost.*

   *"They were very bossy," Little Ghost says. "It served them right! What story are we having next week?"*

   *Big Ghost yawns. "Wait and see, Little Ghost," he says. "Wait and see."*

# WEEK 28

*It's a cold wet night, and Little Ghost slides through the keyhole of the big old house just as fast as he can. He whizzes down the hall and into the warm cosy kitchen … and, just as he'd expected, Big Ghost is yawning on the top of his cupboard. Little Ghost is about to call him when he notices that there are train tracks all over the kitchen floor, and a clockwork train on the table.*

*"What's that?" asks Little Ghost.*

*"Tia and Tim and Jason have been playing trains in here all day," says Big Ghost.*

*"It's not fair," says Little Ghost crossly. "I wish I could play with trains."*

*"I'll tell you a train story instead," says Big Ghost.*

*"It's not the same," says Little Ghost. "I want to play with the children!"*

*Big Ghost shakes his head. "Sorry, Little Ghost … "*

## The Cross Little Train

Train stories are my favourite!

Long ago when I was a little girl trains didn't go *Diddly dee, diddly dum! Diddly dee, diddly dum!* They went *Chuff chuff chuff chuff, chuff chuff chuff chuff!* and clouds of smoke came out of their funnels as they puffed along the railways lines. When they went under bridges or through tunnels they

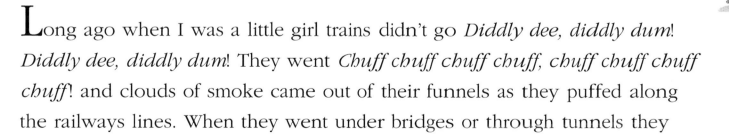

shouted "Whoooooop! Whoooooop!", and as they pulled into the platform they hissed loudly. Sssssssssssss!!! They pulled clattering trucks full of coal, or long carriages full of families, and nearly every town and village had a station nearby.

Most of the trains were quite happy puffing up and down from town to town and village to village, but there was one little train who was always cross. He didn't like going up hills, and he didn't like going down hills. He didn't like pulling trucks, and he didn't like pulling carriages.

"What DO you like?" asked his driver.

"Nothing!" said the cross little train, and he went on huffing and fussing. He stopped halfway up hills, and the trains behind him had to stop too and their trucks bumped into each other and spilt their load of coal. He slid too far along the station platforms, and the passengers had to run to the very end before they could get into the carriages.

He blew clouds of thick white smoke as he whizzed under bridges, and the cars on the road above couldn't see where they were going, and hooted and tooted angrily at the little train.

He went very very slowly indeed when Mrs Johnson and all of Class Three were in a terrible hurry to get to the big town.

"Miss," said Danny Wheeler, "what's wrong with this train?"

"I don't know," said Mrs Johnson, "but if it doesn't hurry up we won't have enough time to go to the shops before we visit the museum."

"Can't we go to the museum another time?" asked Doreen Slater.

"I'm afraid not, Doreen," said Mrs Johnson, and she gave a little sigh.

"Couldn't we go shopping on the way back?" suggested Susan Bannerman.

"We'll only just have time to catch the train back home," said Mrs Johnson.

"Oh no!" said Class Three, and they began to huff and puff just like the cross little train.

Mrs Johnson was right. The train was so late getting into the station that Class Three had to run all the way to the museum. There was not even a spare five minutes for shopping, and Danny Wheeler was very angry indeed. It was his mum's birthday the next day, and he had saved up to buy her the biggest bunch of flowers in the big town flower shop … and now he couldn't. When Class Three came trailing back into the station Danny marched up to the cross little train and stood in front of it with his hands on his hips.

"You're a horrid mean train," Danny said. "You've spoilt our day, and everyone's fed up. Doreen's crying and Susan's grizzling and I can't buy my mum's birthday flowers and it's all your fault. Next time Mrs Johnson says she's taking us to the museum we're all going to ask her if we can come by bus. And we'll tell our mums and dads and they'll go by bus too, and no one will want you, and you'll end up a heap of rust, and it'll serve you right!" And Danny stamped away down the platform.

The cross little train was very surprised. No one had ever spoken to him like that. He was so surprised that he started straight away when his driver asked him to. He quite forgot to huff and fuss, and he chuffed out of the station faster than he'd ever gone before. As he chuffed along he kept thinking "Heap of rust, heap of rust," and he felt more and more and more worried.

"Steady on!" said the little train's driver. "What's got into you today?"

The cross little train didn't answer. "Heap of rust," he said to himself, "heap of rust, heap of rust, heap of rust!" And he panted up the hill without stopping once.

"Hey!" said his driver. "If you keep going like this we'll be too early at the level crossing! Joe won't have shut the gates … slow down!"

"Heap of rust!" moaned the little train, but he began to slow down … and then he saw the flowers. They were growing on the banks either side of the track; pink, white, red … yellow, purple, blue.

SSSSSSSSSSSSSS!!!!! The little train screeched to a stop so suddenly that Doreen and Susan fell off their seats and landed on the floor in a heap. They began to giggle.

Danny snorted loudly. "I told you it was a horrid train," he said. "See? It doesn't care about us."

Mrs Johnson put her head out of the window to see what was going on.

"What's up, miss?" Susan asked. "What's the horrid little train up to now?"

"I'm not sure," Mrs Johnson said. "I can't see why we've stopped. All I can see is flowers."

"Flowers?" Danny hopped up and stuck his head out of a window too. "Miss! They're lovely!" His eyes opened wide. "Hey – miss! Could I pick some? For my mum's birthday present?"

Mrs Johnson shook her head. "We can't get out," she said. "The train might start again."

But the little train didn't start. It stayed exactly where it was. It wouldn't move.

The driver got out of his cab, and went to see what was going on. To his surprise the little train had two rusty tears trickling down its face.

"Have you been crying?" asked the driver. "You'll get rusty if you cry!"

The little train began to cry. "I don't want to be a heap of rust," it said. "I'll be good – I promise! I only stopped so that boy could pick his flowers … tell him he needn't go by bus!"

The driver scratched his head. "Bus? Flowers? Boy? What are you talking about?"

"They're all going to go by bus," snuffled the little train. "It's because I was late … the boy couldn't pick his flowers in the town. But there's flowers here … lots of flowers! Take him some flowers, and I'll go! But if you don't – then I'll cry and cry until I turn into a heap of rust right here!"

The driver scratched his head again. He wasn't at all sure what the little train was worrying about, but he was a kind man. He walked over to the bank, and picked as many of the flowers as he could carry. Then he walked down beside the carriages. Lots of heads were peering out trying to see what was happening.

"Who's got a mum with a birthday tomorrow?" the driver asked. "Anyone here with a mum with a birthday? The train won't go until these are delivered!"

"ME!" yelled Danny. "It's ME! It's my mum's birthday tomorrow – I couldn't buy her flowers 'cos the train was so late!"

"Here you are, then," said the driver, and he handed Danny the flowers.

"Wow!" breathed Danny. "They're the best flowers ever!" He held the flowers tightly, and leant out of the window as far as he could.

"Thanks, little train!" he shouted. "Thank you very very much! And we'll never ever go to town by bus! I promise!"

The little train let out a happy puff of smoke, and the driver hurried back to climb into his cab. The little train started at once … and puffed away down the line so quickly that they reached the level crossing at exactly the right time. They were even one minute early at their home station.

From then on the little train was always good. It puffed happily along up hills and down hills, and it pulled trucks and carriages without complaining. Only the driver noticed that it blew a little extra puff of smoke as it whizzed under bridges … just for old times' sake.

*"Thank you," says Little Ghost as Big Ghost floats back to his cupboard. "And I didn't mean to be cross." He sighs. "But trains do look lots of fun."*

*Big Ghost waves, and as Little Ghost makes his way back into the hall he thinks he hears Big Ghost chuckling …*

# WEEK 29

*Little Ghost is cross again this week. "Mama Ghost wants me home early," he says.*

*"I bet the children here don't have to go to bed early like me."*

*Big Ghost smiles. "Oh yes they do," he says. "I'll tell you exactly how Jason feels!"*

## When Jason Goes to Bed

Nobody says "Time for bed, cat!"
Nobody says, "Time for bed, dog!"
Why do they all say "Time for bed!" to me?

Nobody says "Wash your face. cat!"
Nobody says "Wash your face, dog!"
Why do they all say "Wash your face!" to me?

Nobody says "Brush your teeth, cat!"
Nobody says "Brush your teeth, dog!"
Why do they all say "Brush your teeth to me?"

Nobody says "Hop into bed, cat!"
Nobody says "Hop into bed, dog!"
Why do they all say "Hop into bed to me?"

Nobody says "Give me a kiss, cat!"
Nobody says "Give me a kiss, dog!"
But they all say "Give us a kiss
and we love you lots!" to me!

Little Ghost looks a little ashamed of himself. "That's JUST like me," he says. "Mother Ghost always gives me a kiss goodnight."

"Perhaps you'd better hurry home, then," says Big Ghost. "You don't want to keep Mother Ghost waiting."

"No," says little Ghost, and floats slowly away towards the door ... but then he twirls round, hurries back, and gives Big Ghost a hug. "Goodnight, Big Ghost!"

# WEEK 30

*"Big Ghost! Big Ghost!" Little Ghost is whizzing down the hall just as fast as he can fly. "Big Ghost – I've seen the kitten! The kitten with no name – he was outside the front door! Please will you tell me what happened to him? Tell me about the frog's friend – please!"*

*Big Ghost unfolds himself from the laundry basket in the kitchen. "Sit down, Little Ghost, and I'll begin."*

## The Kitten's Story Part Five

"QUACK!" The kitten woke up with a start. A duck was standing beside him.

"QUACK!" The duck peered at the kitten. "Are you a kitten?"

The kitten nodded.

"Good," said the duck. "Frog says you need to cross the stream."

"Oh, yes please!" said the kitten. "Are you Frog's friend? He pulled me out of the water when I fell in!"

There was a loud splash, and Frog came leaping up the bank.

"Kitten," he said,"this is Duck. Duck, my friend, can you take this young fellow over the stream? He lives in the big green hedge over there."

The duck looked surprised. "I didn't know kittens lived in trees," she said.

The kitten shook his head. "I live under the hedge," he said, "not in it. Can you really take me? I do so want to go home."

"Could he sit on your back, Duck?" asked the frog.

"I think I'd sink," the duck said. "Couldn't he sit on a lily leaf? If he sat on a lily leaf we could push it across."

"Flip my flippers!" said the frog. "What a brain! Two ticks, and I'll be back."

He dived into the water, and swam to a patch of lilies. He chose the biggest leaf, and swam back towing it behind him.

"Here you are, young fellow. Hop on!"

The kitten went nervously down to the edge of the stream. "Ooooooh!" he said, as he felt the lily pad tremble underneath his paws. "I don't like it!"

"Try shutting your eyes," said the frog. "Now, Duck – are you ready? Away we go!"

The kitten shut his eyes tightly. He held his breath as the lily pad moved slowly across the stream. The duck pushed behind, and the frog towed in front.

"Nearly there!" said the frog. "Nearly there!" He gave the lily pad a huge heave.

The lily pad wobbled.

"Meow!" howled the kitten, and he held on as tightly as he could.

"Quack!" said the duck. "Calm down, young kitten. Here we are!"

The kitten felt the lily pad touch the bank with a small bump .

"Oh – meeeeeOW!" he said. He jumped onto dry land, and turned round. "Thank you! Thank you!" he said. "I'll never forget you!"

"No trouble at all!" said the frog, and he and the duck waved as the kitten went hurrying away towards the big green hedge.

"Mother!" the kitten called. "Mother! I'm home!"

There was no answer.

The kitten scampered across the grass – and then stopped and stared.

It wasn't his hedge.

There were sandy holes in among the roots, just like his home, but he knew it was wrong. It was terribly wrong.

The kitten sat down and cried.

"Meeow!" he wailed. "Meeow!"

"Sh!" said a voice. "Sh! You'll wake my babies!"

The kitten spun round.

Behind him was a rabbit. "Oh, please be quiet!" she said. "They've only just gone to sleep!"

"I'm very sorry," said the kitten. "I didn't mean to wake them … but I'm lost!"

"Lost?" The rabbit looked horrified. "But you should be at home! It's getting late!"

"I know," said the kitten, "but this isn't my hedge. I thought it was, but it isn't. It looks just like it – but it's different."

"Silly little thing," said the rabbit. "I expect you've wandered too far up. Or too far down. As long as you stay near the hedge you'll find your home. The hedge goes all the way round the field, you know. Just keep looking." And she popped back down into her hole with a whisk of her white fluffy tail.

"Oh!" The kitten suddenly felt much better. "Oh! I see! If I walk along beside the hedge I'll find our home and Mother for certain!"

Pop! The rabbit was back out.

"A little thing like you really shouldn't be out so late," she said. "Quick! Creep down here, and you can stay for the night. You can find your home in the morning. Can't have you wandering about in the dark – I wouldn't sleep a wink for worrying! Come along down – and mind you tiptoe. I don't want those babies woken up!"

The kitten didn't argue. It was getting very dark, and there were strange rustly noises that made him shiver. He tiptoed after the rabbit, and found himself in a warm burrow filled with soft grass.

"There!" she said. "No nonsense, now – clean your whiskers and go to sleep. You'll find your mother in the morning."

"Thank you," whispered the kitten. He snuggled down in the grass … and three little baby bunnies snored and snuffled beside him.

"I'll find Mother in the morning," the kitten told himself. "And she'll tell me about our very special place … our home which is warm and cosy … where we'll be hugged …" He began to purr.

"Sh!" said the rabbit, but she said it very softly.

Turn to page 180 for the next part of the kitten's story.

*Little Ghost gives a long sigh of pleasure. "That is so lovely," he says. "Does the kitten find his mother very soon?"*

*"Maybe," says Big Ghost. "But I can hear your mother outside – she's calling for you down the chimney!"*

*Little Ghost gets up from the laundry basket. "See you soon, Big Ghost," he says.*

I like playing in the garden.

# WEEK 31

"Boo!" Little Ghost pops his head over the edge of the wheelbarrow.

"Hello," says Big Ghost. "I wondered if you'd find me here!"

"It's so hot tonight," says Little Ghost. "Please will you tell me a garden story? A story about all the children in the garden?"

Big Ghost moves up so that there's room for Little Ghost on top of the weeds.

"I'll tell you a Daisy B story," he says.

## Spots!

It was a fine day. Ross and Tim and Tia were playing football. Jason was digging a hole. Granny Annie was picking flowers. Mum was pulling up weeds. Julius was dozing in a deckchair with a cup of tea. Daisy B was sniffing the roses.

It was all very quiet and peaceful, when suddenly –
"WAAAAAAAH!"

Daisy B burst into very loud and noisy tears.

Ross missed the ball and fell over.

Tia and Tim ran into each other with a Bump!

Jason dropped his spade.

Granny Annie scattered flowers all over the grass.

Mum stung herself on a nettle.

Julius leapt up from his deckchair and spilt his tea.

"What's the matter, Daisy B?" he said. "Are you hurt?"

Daisy B was sobbing. "POOR beetle," she wept. "POOR beetle."

"Has she been stung?" asked Ross.

"Is it a wasp?" asked Tia and Tim.

"She's always crying," said Jason.

"Poor little girl," said Granny Annie.

"Where does it hurt?" asked Mum.

"What beetle?" asked Julius.

Daisy B was still crying. She was sniffing loudly, and tears were running down her cheeks.

"Poor poor beetle," she wailed, "poor beetle's ill. Beetle's got spots."

She held out her fat little hand.

"Make him better," she said. "Make poor beetle better."

Everyone hurried to look – and there was a ladybird.

"Daisy B," said Tia, "that's a ladybird. Ladybirds always look like that."

Daisy B peered closely at her ladybird, her tears dried up as if by magic.

"Hello, ladybird," she said.

The ladybird stretched its wings … and flew away home.

"WAAAAAA!" howled Daisy B.

*"Do ladybirds always have spots?" Little Ghost asks.*

*"Yes," says Big Ghost. "At least, I think they do."*

*Little Ghost laughs, jumps off the wheelbarrow – and freezes. "Big Ghost," he says, "what's that noise? Is it the rabbits?"*

*"It's the guinea pig," Big Ghost tells him. "It's crunching up its carrots."*

*"Can you – " Little Ghost begins, but Big Ghost interrupts him.*

*"I know," he says, "and the answer's yes. We'll have a guinea pig story next week."*

*"Hurrah!" says Little Ghost, and he spins away under the stars.*

# WEEK 32

*"Guinea pig, guinea pig, guinea pig!" sings Little Ghost as he flies down to the garden.*

*Big Ghost is sitting on top of the guinea pig's hutch, and Little Ghost lands beside him, smiling happily.*

*"Ready?" says Big Ghost. "Then I'll begin!"*

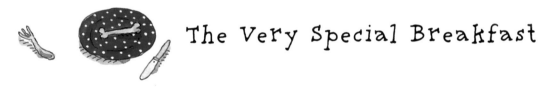 ## The Very Special Breakfast

There was once a guinea pig, and his name was Toffee. He lived with his mum and his dad and his five big sisters, and he was fussy about his food.

"Come along, Toffee dear," said his mum. "Eat your nice breakfast."

"Don't like cabbage," said Toffee.

"Have a carrot," said his dad.

"Don't like carrot," said Toffee.

"You can have some of our potato peelings," said his sisters.

"Don't like potato peelings," said Toffee. "I want ice cream. And cake. And chocolate biscuits."

"But ice cream and cake and chocolate biscuits aren't good for little guinea pigs," said his mum.

"Don't care," said Toffee, and he pattered off to see what he could find.

Toffee went to see the dog.

"What do you eat for breakfast?" he asked.

"Bones," said the dog. "Meaty bones."

"Don't like bones," said Toffee, and he pattered away.

Toffee went to see the cat.

"What do you eat for breakfast?" he asked.

"Fish," said the cat. "Slippery silver fish."

"Don't like fish," said Toffee, and he pattered away.

Toffee went pattering down the path and out into the wide wide world.

He hadn't gone too far when he met a fox.

Be careful Toffee!

161

"Good morning," said the fox, and he smiled a toothy smile. "And where are you off to in such a hurry?"

"I'm looking for my breakfast," said Toffee. "What do foxes eat?"

The fox looked at Toffee, and he licked his lips. "All kinds of things," he said. "What do you like eating?"

"Ice cream," said Toffee, "and cake. And chocolate biscuits."

"Goodness me," said the fox. "That's just exactly what I was going to have for my breakfast. Why don't you come and have breakfast with me?"

"Yes please," said Toffee, and he pattered along with the fox.

When they reached the fox's den the fox opened the front door.

"DO come in," he said.

Toffee hurried in, and three little fox cubs jumped up to see what was going on.

"Daddy Fox, Daddy Fox – did you bring us our breakfast?" they asked.

"Guess what, my dears," said Daddy Fox. "This little fellow has come to have breakfast with us. He's come to share our ice cream. And cake. And chocolate biscuits. Isn't that lovely?" And he winked at his three little fox cubs. The three little fox cubs winked back.

"Yum yum YUM!" they said.

"Now, my dears," said Daddy Fox, "I'll just run and fetch Mummy Fox, and then we'll all sit down and have a delicious breakfast together."

And he hurried out of the door.

Toffee looked round the den. It was very dark, and very messy.

"What are those?" asked Toffee.

"Feathers," said the first little fox cub.

"Feathers?" said Toffee. He began to feel uncomfortable.

"Our mother's been stuffing pillows," said the first little fox cub.

"Oh," said Toffee. He couldn't see any pillows, but he could see something else …

"What's that?" asked Toffee.

"Fur," said the second little fox cub.

"Fur?" said Toffee. He began to feel nervous.

"Our mother's been sewing a fur coat," said the second little fox cub.

"Oh," said Toffee. He couldn't see a fur coat anywhere, but he could see something else …

"OH!" Toffee stared, and his teeth began to chatter. "W … w … what are those?"

"BONES!" said the littlest fox cub. "Yum yum YUM!"

"Ssh!" said his brothers – but it was too late. Toffee jumped up and ran through the door.

The three little fox cubs chased after him calling "Come back! Come back!" but Toffee didn't stop.

He ran and he ran and he ran and he ran … all the way back to his own little house. He rushed through the front door, and he slammed it shut behind him.

"Toffee!" said his mum. "You've come back!"

"Yes," said Toffee. "And I'm hungry. And I don't want ice cream. Or cake. Or chocolate biscuits. Can I have some cabbage? And a carrot? And some potato peelings? PLEASE?"

*Little Ghost is laughing so much he falls off the top of the guinea pig's hutch.*

*"Are you all right?" asks Big Ghost anxiously.*

*"Yes!" Little Ghost floats up on the other side. "Hey, Big Ghost – is that Toffee in the hutch?"*

*"Well … " Big Ghost scratches his head. "It might be. He is called Toffee … "*

*"Don't forget to go on eating carrots, Toffee!" Little Ghost says, and he's still laughing as he floats up to join Mother Ghost on the rooftop.*

# WEEK 33

It's foggy tonight, and Mama Ghost makes sure that little Ghost goes down the right chimneypot.

"See you soon," says Little Ghost, and disappears.

"Cooee! Big Ghost!" he calls as he flutters out into the playroom.

Big Ghost stretches.

"Do you want a tiger story, Little Ghost?" he asks. "Tim and Daisy B have been playing animal safari parks all afternoon."

"Yes please," says Little Ghost.

## The Tiger who couldn't Roar

There was once a tiger who couldn't roar.

When it was time for roaring lessons Little Tiger One Stripe roared a great big roar. "Grrrrrrr!!!"

Little Tiger Two Stripes roared an even bigger roar. "GRRRR!"

Little Tiger Three Stripes roared a huge huge roar that made the little green parrots shake on the top of the coconut tree. "GRRRRRRRR!"

Little Tiger Four Stripes roared such a great big roar that the little green parrots flew far far away. "GRRRRR!"

165

But when Fiver tried to roar all that came out was a little squeak. "Eeek."

Old Tiger looked cross. "Fiver," he said. "That is no noise for a tiger. Please roar properly."

But Tiger couldn't. "Eeek," he said sadly, "Eeek. Eeek. Arrrk. Eeek."

The other little tigers began to laugh.

"You sound like a mouse," said Little Tiger One Stripe.

"You couldn't scare a rabbit," said Little Tiger Two Stripes.

"You couldn't scare anything!" giggled Little Tiger Three Stripes.

"Squeak squeak squeaky!" sniggered Little Tiger Four Stripes. "Mind an owl doesn't catch you!"

Fiver's whiskers drooped, and a tear trickled down his nose.

When the roaring lesson was over one, two, three, four stripy little tigers bounced and pounced away. Fiver trailed behind them.

"Let's play hide and seek!" said Little Tiger One Stripe. "I'll go into the jungle and roar – and you can find me!"

"I want to go into the jungle and roar too," said Little Tiger Two Stripes.

"And me!" said Little Tiger Three Stripes.

"And I'll come and find you!" said Little Tiger Four Stripes.

"Can I play?" asked Fiver.

His four little brothers looked at each other.

"No," said Little Tiger Two Stripes. "You can't roar and tell us that you're coming to find us."

"And you can't roar when you do find us," said Little Tiger One Stripe.

"Oh," said Fiver, and he went to sit behind a rock.

The four little brothers hopped and skipped away into the forest.

Fiver sat behind his rock and sighed.

"I'm no good at being a tiger," he thought. "I'll go away. I'll go into the jungle and I won't come back." And he padded away between the trees.

He hadn't gone far when he heard a noise.

"Eeek! Squeak! Help! Eeek! Eeek!"

Fiver looked round.

A mouse was scampering up the path behind him as fast as she could go. A long spotty snake was slithering along behind her.

"Sssss!" hissed the snake. "Come and be my breakfast, little moussssse!"

Fiver took a deep breath. "I'm a no good tiger," he said to himself. "I don't mind if a snake eats me for his breakfast. I just don't care!" and he jumped at the snake.

"Eeek! Arrrk! Eeeek!" he squeaked.

The snake stopped and stared.

"What did you just ssssay?" it asked.

"Eeek!" said Fiver. "Leave that mouse alone!"

The snake stared a moment longer, and then it began to laugh. It laughed so much that it tied itself up in a knot, and still it went on laughing.

"What a funny little tiger!" it chortled. "A tiger that squeaksss like a moussse! Tee hee hee tee hee! That's so funny I don't mind losing my breakfassssst!" And it untied itself and went sliding away into the bushes.

Fiver sat down. He found he was glad that the snake hadn't eaten him – but he still didn't like being laughed at.

"Eeek!" It was the mouse. "Thank you so much!"

Fiver looked down. "It was nothing," he said.

The mouse came a little closer. "What's the matter? You've just saved me from a terrible snake! Aren't you pleased?"

"No," said Fiver. "I'm a no good tiger. I can't roar. I can only squeak."

The mouse looked a little offended. "There's nothing wrong with squeaking," she said.

Fiver tried to smile. "Oh, I'm sorry," he said. "I didn't mean to be rude. But mice squeak. Tigers are meant to roar."

"You did a very brave thing with only a squeak," said the mouse, and she pattered away into the grass.

"Grrrrr! GRRRR! Grrrrrr!"

Fiver jumped up. He could hear his brothers roaring.

"Grrrrr! GRRRR! Grrrrrr."

There it was again … and then there was a rustling and a crashing and three of his little brothers tumbled out of the bushes beside him.

"Quick! Quick!" they puffed. "There's a long spotty snake, and it's trying to catch Little Tiger Four Stripes for its breakfast! Run! Run! Run! We must fetch Old Tiger at once!"

Fiver looked at them in surprise. "A long spotty snake?" he said. "That won't hurt anyone!"

"Oh, it will!" said Little Tiger One Stripe. "It's hissing and opening its mouth wide wide WIDE!"

And the three little tigers rushed away between the trees.

Fiver stood very still and listened. The jungle was very quiet. Very quiet indeed.

"Eeek! Aaark!" squeaked Fiver. "Mouse – can you hear me?"

"Of course I can," said the mouse. "There's no need to shout!"

Fiver saw her sitting near his paws.

"Do you know where my brother is?" he asked.

The mouse nodded. "He'll make a spotty snake's dinner if you don't hurry up," she said. "This way!" And she scampered off.

Fiver hurried after her. In and out of the trees they went … and there was a tall tree with a frightened little tiger balancing on the very top branch. The long spotty snake was slithering nearer … and nearer … and nearer … when –

"EEEK! AARK! EEEK!" squeaked Fiver, and began scrambling up the tree after the snake.

The snake looked down at Fiver. "Ssssss!" it hissed. "It won't work this time. I'm on my way to catch my delicioussss tiger dinner! Go away, squeaky!"

Fiver's whiskers twitched.

Fiver began to feel angry.

Fiver began to feel very angry.

Fiver began to feel very angry indeed.

He stopped climbing, and he opened his mouth, and he – ROARED!

He roared so loudly that the tree shivered all over. The leaves trembled, the branches shook – and the long spotty snake slipped and slid and fell to the ground with a THUMP!

"OUCH!" it hissed crossly, and slithered away as fast as it could go.

Little Tiger Four Stripes and Fiver scrambled down the tree, and they hurried home together – and met Old Tiger and their three brothers at the edge of the jungle.

"Fiver saved me!" shouted Little Tiger Four Stripes. "He roared so loudly that the long spotty snake fell out of the tree! He's a hero – and he's got the loudest roar of all of us!"

"Well done," said Old Tiger. "Well done, Fiver. You're a brave little tiger. Show us how you roar!"

And Fiver opened his mouth and roared. "Eee! Aark! Eeek!"

*"I'm going to roar at Mama Ghost when I go up the chimney," says Little Ghost.*

*"Don't frighten her," says Big Ghost, and he settles back down in the toybox. "Good night, Little Ghost."*

*"Good night, Big Ghost."*

# WEEK 34

*Little Ghost is looking all over the house for Big Ghost,
but there's no sign of him. Little Ghost is about to give
up when he floats into the sitting room - and there's Big Ghost
fast asleep on the mantelpiece.*

*"I couldn't find you," says Little Ghost. "I thought you'd gone away!"*

*"Sorry," says Big Ghost. "I was talking to the goldfish, and I fell asleep. I thought
I'd tell you a goldfish story!"*

## Swim swim swim

I'm a little goldfish swimming round

Round and round and round and round and round

I'm a little goldfish singing as I swim

Round and round and round
Round and round and round
What do I sing as I'm swimming round and round
Round and round and round
Round and round and round?
Here's what I sing as I'm swimming round and round
Round and round and round
Round and round and round –
I'm a little goldfish swimming round and round
Round and round and round
Round and round and round …..

"I'm not surprised you went to sleep," says Little Ghost. "Who does he belong to?"

"He's Jason's goldfish," says Big Ghost. "But all the family look after him."

"Will you tell me a story about Jason next week?" says Little Ghost.

"If you want," says Big Ghost.

"I do!" says Little Ghost.

# WEEK 35

*Big Ghost and Little Ghost are in the kitchen this week, snuggled up in the laundry basket.*

*"Go on, then," says Little Ghost. "You said you'd tell me a story about Jason."*

## Jason's Good Idea

The car wouldn't start.

"Oh dear!" said Mum. "I need to go shopping!"

"I'll have a look at it later," said Julius. "Poor old thing. Nobody ever looks after it."

"It's very dirty," said Jason.

"Hey!" said Ross. "I'll clean it!"

"OK," said Julius. "But don't let Jason get wet."

"I'll just watch," said Jason.

Ross began cleaning the car.

Jason stood and watched.

"I can help you," he said. "I like cleaning cars."

Ross shook his head. "No," he said. "You'll get too wet."

"I won't," said Jason.

"Go away," said Ross.

Jason didn't go away. He watched Ross pour water over the bonnet. Swoosh!

He watched Ross washing the bonnet with a sponge. Swish, swish, swish!

Drip! Drip! Drip! Water dripped everywhere.

Jason sighed. He loved playing with water.

"Can I help a little bit?" he asked. "I promise I won't get wet."

"You will," said Ross. "Go away."

Jason didn't go away. He went on watching. He watched Ross pour water over the wheels. Splash!

He watched Ross scrubbing the wheels. Scrub, scrub, scrub.

"Bother!" said Ross.

"What's the matter?" asked Jason.

"The wheels are really dirty," Ross said. "I need a scrubbing brush."

"I'll get it!" said Jason.

"OK," said Ross. "Thanks."

Jason rushed into the house.

"Mum!" he said. "Ross wants a scrubbing brush!"

"It's in the bathroom," said Mum.

Jason dashed upstairs. The scrubbing brush was on the edge of the bath.

Jason grabbed it, and then he stopped. He looked at the rows of bottles and pots on the bathroom shelf.

"Cleaning stuff!" he said, and he took down a pink bottle.

Jason gave Ross the scrubbing brush.

"Thanks," said Ross.

"I've got some cleaning stuff too," said Jason.

"Great," said Ross. "Pour it in the bucket."

Jason took the top off the bottle and poured.

There was a wonderful smell of roses.

"Smells nice," said Ross. "Thanks, Jason."

Jason glowed. "I'm helpful, aren't I?" he asked.

"Yes," said Ross.

"So can I have just a little go with the sponge?" Jason asked. "If I promise I won't get wet?"

Ross sighed. "OK. Just a wipe or two."

Jason dunked the sponge into the bucket and squeezed.

Bubbles burst out, shiny, shimmery cascades of bubbles.

"Hey!" said Ross. "What's going on?"

Jason splooshed the sponge on the car. Bubbles flew everywhere.

"Yippee!" said Jason, and squeezed the sponge again. Bubbly foam spattered in all directions.

"Stop it!" said Ross, but Jason couldn't stop. It was too much fun. He squeezed and he splooshed and he splooshed and he squeezed. There were bubbles in his hair and on his clothes, and bubbles all over the car, and bubbles floating in the air.

"Catch them!" shouted Jason, and he jumped to catch a bubble.

CRASH! The bucket fell over with a crash and a splash.

"Jason!" yelled Ross. "I'm soaked!"

Mum came running out of the house. "Whatever's going on?" she said. "Jason – you're soaking wet! And look at the car! And Ross – you're sopping too – OH!"

Mum stopped, and stared at the pink bottle lying on the ground.

"My rose bath oil!" she said. "Oh no! You NAUGHTY boys!"

"It's only cleaning stuff," said Jason.

"That," said Mum, "is my very special most expensive simply wonderful essence of roses bubble bath oil that Granny gave me for my birthday," and she sounded very cross indeed.

"Oh," said Jason.

"Sorry," said Ross.

Jason looked at the car.

The bubbles had dripped off, and it was shining in the sunshine.

"Wow!" he said. "I bet our car feels very special if it's got simply wonderful rose smell all over it. I bet it'll start now!"

"I bet it won't," said Mum. But it did.

And it smelt of simply wonderful roses for a whole week.

*As Little Ghost gets slowly out of the basket, there is a pit pat of small furry feet, and the kitten with no name comes in. He sees Big Ghost and Little Ghost, and begins to purr.*

*"Hello, kitten!" says Little Ghost. "Have you got a name yet?"*

*"I don't think he has," says Big Ghost.*

*"I wish I could find you one," says Little Ghost. "It must be strange not having a name," and he strokes the kitten before he flies off up the chimney.*

# WEEK 36

*Little Ghost is still thinking about the kitten with no name when he arrives for his story.*

*"What happened to him after he stayed with the rabbits?" he asks Big Ghost.*

*"I'll tell you," says Big Ghost, and he and Little Ghost get comfortable on top of Daisy B's woolly cardigan.*

## The Kitten with no Name: Part Six

The kitten woke up feeling bright and cheerful. The three bunny babies were still fast asleep, but Mother Rabbit was bustling about tidying up.

"There's a good little kitten," she said when she saw him beginning to wash his paws.

"Now, when you've finished washing you can come and have some breakfast, and then you must run along and find your mother. She must be worried sick about you!"

The kitten nodded, and gave his paws one last lick.

"I'm ready!" he said. "And I'm hungry!"

"That's good," said the rabbit, and she gave him a very small carrot.

The kitten's whiskers drooped.

"Oh," he said as politely as he could. "Thank you."

He tried hard to eat the carrot, but he didn't like it much.

"There there," said the rabbit as she swept up the bits. "I expect you're missing your mother."

"Yes," said the kitten, and he nodded hard.

The rabbit patted his head. "Time to run along," she said. "Make certain you keep going the same way, and you're sure to find your home. Don't go talking to any strange animals, and keep near the hedge!"

"I will," said the kitten. He looked round the burrow. It suddenly felt very warm and cosy, and the world outside seemed very big.

"Now now," said the rabbit, "you'll be fine."

"Yes," said the kitten. "And thank you very very much for looking after me."

The rabbit looked pleased. "It was a pleasure," she said, and she waved as the kitten scrambled up and out of the sandy burrow.

Outside it was a chilly grey day. The kitten shivered, and then shook himself.

181

"I'll soon be home now!" he said. "I'll keep close to the hedge, and I'll be there in no time at all. Won't Mother be pleased to see me! We can snuggle up and have breakfast together. Mew! I'm *so* hungry!" And he began to hurry along, purring as he went.

"Cuckoo! Cuckoo! Cuckoo! Help me! Help! Oh, won't anyone help me?"

The kitten froze. The voice was coming from above him, high up in the hedge.

"Please! Please help me!"

The kitten peered up between the leaves. A feather floated past his nose, and he sneezed. "ATCHOOO!"

"Cuckoo! Help me! Please!"

The kitten shook the feather off. "Meeow! I'm coming!" he called, and he began to wriggle in between the twigs and the branches. They grew closely together, and there wasn't much room for even a skinny kitten.

"Ow!" he said. "Ouch! Meeow!" But he kept struggling upwards until

POP!

Out he came at the top.

"Oh no!" said the voice, "you're a CAT! Oh no – now I'll be eaten and Father will be *furious*!"

The kitten opened his eyes very wide.

A big blue grey bird was lying flat on his back in a neat little nest. His legs were waving in the air, and he was trying to flap his wings – but he was, very definitely, stuck.

"Whatever are you doing?" asked the kitten.

"Can't you see?" said the bird crossly. "I'm stuck! I've been here for ages, and I can't move. Hurry up and eat me."

"But I don't want to eat you," said the kitten. "I came to help you."

"Are you sure?" The bird sounded surprised.

"Quite sure," the kitten said. "What can I do?"

The bird waved his legs again. "Pull me out, of course," he said. "I told my dad I needed a bigger nest, but he just wouldn't listen. He said he and Mum had always made them this size, and it was my fault for growing so big. Here, grab a leg and heave!"

The kitten balanced himself on a branch, and took hold of one of the blue grey bird's skinny scaly legs.

"I'll count to three," said the bird. "Ready? One – two – three – pull!"

The kitten pulled – and heaved – and hauled – and –
CRASH!

The bird shot out of the nest and he and the kitten tumbled down to the ground in a flurry of leaves and feathers.

"OUCH!" said the kitten, and he rubbed his head. The bird began to strut about, shaking his feathers.

"Coo!" he said, "did you see me fly?"

"Er … yes," said the kitten.

"I'm a star at flying!" said the bird. "Cuckoo! Cuckoo! Best flyer ever – that's me! Cuckoo bird, and pleased to meet you. Coo – I'd better go and find Mum and Dad!"

"Yes," said the kitten, and he rubbed his head again.

The cuckoo peered at the kitten with his beady black eyes. "Hey – what's up with you? And what are you doing round here anyway?"

"I'm going home too," said the kitten. He sighed. "I'm just not quite sure which way home is."

The cuckoo hopped up onto a twig. "Why didn't you say? I'll find it for you! I'll fly up in the air. Cuckoo! I can see everything from up there!"

The kitten sat down. "Oooh yes! Yes, you could!"

"So what am I looking for?" asked the cuckoo.

"A hedge," said the kitten. "A hedge like this one."

The cuckoo clicked his beak. "Tut tut! There are hedges everywhere!" he said. "Why don't I look for your mother?"

The kitten nodded. "That would be good."

The cuckoo hopped up to a higher twig. "So what does she look like?"

"Like me," said the kitten, stripy with white paws. And she's got a white tip to her tail. Just like me!"

"Easy!" said the cuckoo. "You wait here. I'll be off and have a fly around. I'll be back in no time."

"Thank you," said the kitten.

Cuckoo bird hopped higher up the hedge. "See you soon!" he said, and he stretched his wings. "Here I go! Cuckoo!" And the kitten saw him stagger, and then flap steadily up and up into the sky.

The kitten watched until the cuckoo was a small speck, and then he curled up in the dead leaves.

"I hope he finds Mother soon," he thought. "I do miss her so much. And I'm so SO hungry. But maybe she's found the very special place for us to live … our very special place where we'll be loved and hugged … and live for ever and ever … "

And the kitten began to dream a happy dream.

*"That kitten has met a lot of interesting animals," says Little Ghost. "But I do hope he finds his mother soon." He suddenly has a dreadful thought, and sits up very straight. "He does find his mother, doesn't he?"*

*"You don't need to worry too much," Big Ghost says. "Now, off you go to your mother."*

# WEEK 37

*Big Ghost is in the playroom this evening. Little Ghost finds him asleep on top of a heap of soft toys.*

*"Wake up, Big Ghost!" he calls.*

*Big Ghost opens his eyes. "Ooooh," he yawns. "I was very comfortable!"*

*Little Ghost points at a stiff-looking bear sitting by himself.*

*"Who's that?" he asks.*

*"Oh, that's a very special bear," says Big Ghost.*

## The Big Bold Bear

There was once a big bold bear. He had shiny black eyes, a smart red bow and a string in the middle of his back. When the string was pulled the bear growled,

GRRRR! GRRRR! GRRRR!

He lived on the top shelf of a little boy's bedroom, and he never came down. The big bold bear thought it was because he was so special, but the real reason was that the little boy didn't like him. The bear was too hard to cuddle, and his growl was scary. He had a cross face, and his eyes were hard and shiny like beads. Mostly the little boy forgot he was there at all, and the big bold bear sat on his shelf and grew dusty.

The little boy grew older, and taller. He stopped playing with soft toys and dolls, and began to want dinosaurs and aeroplanes and tin trucks and diggers. There were two new babies in the house now, a baby boy and a baby girl, and the boy went to look at them in their cots.

"They're the little ones now, aren't they?" he asked.

His mum nodded, and gave him a kiss.

"Then they can have my teddies," the boy said.

"Are you sure, Ross?" Mum asked.

"Yes," Ross said. "Oh – and they can have the big teddy too." He took Mum's hand and pulled her into his room. He pointed at the big bold bear. "That one."

Mum reached up and took the big bold bear down from the shelf.

"I'd forgotten all about this one," she said. "He doesn't look very friendly, does he?"

"No," said Ross, and he made a face at the bear. "Throw him away!"

Mum went on looking at the bear. She turned him over, and pulled his string.

GRRRR! GRRRR! GRRRR!

went the big bold bear. Mum laughed. "Scary!" she said. "Maybe I'll take him to one of the charity shops." And she took the bear away and left him in a dark corner of the kitchen. He slipped down behind the vegetable rack, and there he stayed.

Ross went on growing, and so did the twins.

Tim was a good baby, and he hardly ever cried. Tia was a noisy baby. She cried nearly all the time, and no one knew why.

"Wind," said Granny Annie, but no amount of patting and rocking stopped Tia crying.

"Perhaps she's hungry?" said Mum, but however much milk Tia was given she still went on wailing.

Isn't Tia a noisy baby!

Everyone grew very very tired of the noise. Mum always looked worn out. Granny Annie always looked anxious. Ross was always fed up. Only Tim seemed to take no notice. He slept happily through all the crying.

One evening it seemed to be worse than ever before. Tim was fast asleep, but Tia had howled and bawled all day long without stopping once. It felt as if the whole house was full of noise, and even the dogs crept under the table with their tails between their legs.

"Maybe she'd like some music," said Granny Annie.

"Maybe you should send her back," said Ross.

"I'll give her some warm milk," said Mum, but Tia waved her little arms so wildly that she knocked the bottle out of Mum's hand. It rolled away under the vegetable rack, and Ross went to fetch it. Tia screamed even louder than before.

"Oh, look!" said Ross. "Look what I've found!"

He had moved the rack to find the bottle, and found the big bold bear. But the bear was not nearly as smart as he had been. His bow was faded pink, and his eyes no longer shone.

"Oh, don't bring that out," said Mum. "It'll scare Tia to bits. Put it back, Ross."

Mum was too late. Ross had already pulled the bear's string.

GRRRR!!! GRRRR!!! GRRRR!!! went the bear.

Tia stopped crying.

There was a sudden silence.

Ross pulled the string again.

GRRRR!!! GRRRR!!! GRRRR!!!

There was a strange little chuckling sound that no one had ever heard before.

Mum gasped. Granny Annie held her breath.

"Look!" Ross said. "Tia's laughing!"

And she was. Tia was laughing, and holding out her fat little arms for the big bold bear, and when he was tucked up beside her in her cot she shut her eyes and went peacefully to sleep. She slept all that night, and when she woke up in the morning she smiled and smiled and smiled as she ate her breakfast.

"Well I never," said Mum.

"Isn't that a miracle?" said Granny Annie.

"Yes," said Ross, and he pulled the big bold bear's string.

GRRRR!!! GRRRR!!! GRRRR!!!

went the bear, and Tia laughed and laughed
and laughed …

and Tim woke up and howled and howled and howled.

*Little Ghost gives the big bold bear a closer look.*

*"He must be quite old if he belonged to Ross and then Tia," he says. "Do they still play with him?"*

*"Tia still loves him best," says Big Ghost. "He's usually on the end of her bed."*

*"Oh," says Little Ghost, and he gives the big bold bear a pat.*

*"GRRRR!" says the bear, and Little Ghost jumps.*

*"I think I'll go home now," he says, and he whizzes away up the chimney calling "Mama Ghost! Mama Ghost! Are you there?"*

# WEEK 38

*Big Ghost is waiting for Little Ghost in the hallway.*

*"Are you all right, Little Ghost?" he asks.*

*"Of course I am," says Little Ghost.*

*"Good," says Big Ghost. "Only I thought you were frightened by the big bold bear."*

*"Not me," says Little Ghost, but then he hesitates. "Well … only a very little bit."*

*"I'll tell you about a fly tonight," says Big Ghost. "And there's no growling in the story!"*

## The Fly Who Always Knew Best

There was once a horrid little fly who always knew best.

Whenever anyone told him anything he always knew better.

When his friends said, "It's very cold today," the little fly said, "Yes, but I know something you don't know. I know that it's very cold today because a great big green elephant has taken the sun away to warm his toes."

When his friends said, "It's very hot today," the little fly said, "Yes, but I know something you don't know. I know that it's very hot today because the great big green elephant has tossed the sun back into the sky."

When his friends said, "It's very windy today," the little fly said, "Yes, but I know something you don't know. I know that it's very windy today because that great big green elephant has a dreadful cold and keeps on sneezing."

When his friends said, "We know one thing. We know that spiders spin webs to catch little flies," the little fly said, "No no NO! You don't know ANYTHING! I know that spiders spin webs for the great big green elephant to dance on! And I can dance on it too!"

Then the horrid little fly flew straight into a spider's web …

… and the spider wrapped him up in a bundle and ate him for her tea.

*Little Ghost laughs loudly. "Didn't that serve the fly right?" he says.*

*"I think it did," says Big Ghost.*

*"There's a fly up there in the corner," says Little Ghost. "Do you think it knows about spiders?"*

*"I expect so," says Big Ghost.*

*"Good," says Little Ghost. "Can we have a story about a BIG animal next week? And can I meet you in the playroom?"*

*"I'll see you there," says Big Ghost.*

# WEEK 39

*Big Ghost isn't in the playroom when Little Ghost goes to look for him; he's sitting on the very top of the stairs, near Granny Annie's attic room. Toy animals are neatly arranged in twos on every step.*

*"Hello," says Little Ghost, "what are you doing here?"*

*"I was watching Jason and Granny Annie playing Noah's Ark." says Big Ghost.*

*"Oh," says Little Ghost, and he looks at the animals. "Will you tell me my big animal story now?"*

*"Is a lion big enough?" asks Big Ghost, and Little Ghost nods.*

## The Grumpy Lion

Long long long ago there was a lion who was not at all a nice lion. He was grumpy, he was bossy, and he hated sharing anything with anybody. He lived all alone in a great big beautiful cave, and he sat in the doorway and grumbled and rumbled whenever any other animals went past.

"Look at that! The elephants are tramping through MY grass!"

"It's just not good enough. Those giraffes are eating MY leaves."

"Oh me oh my. The monkeys are swinging from MY creepers!"

The lion was never ever pleased to see anyone, so when a small white mouse came skipping up to his cave he frowned a terrible frown and he roared a terrible roar.

"What do you want, little mouse? Run away or I'll eat you for my dinner!"

The mouse sat up and twirled his tail.

"Actually," he said, "I was looking for somewhere to live. I heard you had a great big beautiful cave, and I thought you might like to share it with me. I'm very small, and I don't take up much room – and I'm very good at telling jokes."

The lion frowned even more fiercely. "WHAT?" he roared, and his roar made the leaves shiver on the trees. "Me share my great big beautiful cave with a mouse? Certainly not! Not ever! Never never never! NO!"

"Oh well," said the mouse, "if that's the way you feel about it I'll be off. Sorry to have bothered you!" And he skipped away into the jungle.

The lion sat in his doorway and raged to himself. "A mouse! A horrible mouse – and he wants to live in my great big beautiful cave! How dare he? The cheek of it!" And the lion grew angrier and angrier, until he thought he would burst. He saw the elephants tramping through the grass, and he roared out loud,

"Hey! Elephants! A horrible squeaky mouse wants to come and live with me in my great big beautiful cave! Have you ever heard of anything so dreadful?"

The elephants stopped and looked at the lion.

"A mouse? Wanting to live with you?" they said. "Well, bless our trunks and tails! He must be a very strange mouse! We wouldn't want to live with you. Certainly not. You're much too grumpy." And they went tramping on their way.

The lion sat down again in his doorway. "Whatever do they mean?" he said. "I'm not grumpy. I'm ANGRY, and it's all because of that horrible squeaky cheeky mouse." And he grumbled and he rumbled until he saw the giraffes eating the leaves, and he roared out very loudly,

"Hey! Giraffes! A horrible squeaky cheeky skittery mouse wants to come and live with me in my great big beautiful cave! Have you ever heard of anything so dreadful?"

The giraffes stopped eating and looked at the lion.

"A mouse? Wanting to live with you?" they said. "Well, bless our big brown patches! He must be a very strange mouse! We wouldn't want to live with you. Not ever. You're much too bossy." And they went on eating the leaves.

The lion sat down again in his doorway. "Whatever do they mean?" he said. "I'm not bossy. I'm ANGRY, and it's all because of that horrible squeaky cheeky skittery scattery mouse." And he grumbled and he rumbled until he saw the monkeys swinging on the vines, and he roared out very loudly indeed,

"Hey! Monkeys! A horrible squeaky cheeky skittery scattery pattery mouse wants to come and live with me in my great big beautiful cave! Have you ever heard of anything so dreadful?"

The monkeys stopped swinging and looked at the lion.

"A mouse? And he wants to live with you?" they said. "Well, bless our ears and noses! He must be the strangest mouse that ever there was! We wouldn't want to live with you. Never never never. You hate sharing anything with anybody." And they swung away and away through the trees.

The lion sat down again in his doorway. "Whatever do they mean?" he said. "The elephants said they wouldn't want to live with me. The giraffes said they didn't want to either. And the monkeys said he must be the strangest mouse ever if he wants to live in my great big beautiful cave … oh, my teeth and whiskers! I do believe nobody likes me! Nobody likes me at all!"

And a big tear trickled down the lion's nose, and he felt very sorry for himself.

Now the lion is sad what will happen next?

"Perhaps I should have let that little white mouse share my great big beautiful cave after all," he said sadly. "Maybe his jokes would cheer me up, but it's too late now. I sent him away. I expect he's gone to live with the elephants. Or the giraffes. Or the monkeys."

"No such thing!" said a small squeaky voice. "Here I am!"

And there was the little white mouse, with a bag on his back.

"Oh!" said the lion. "Do please come in!"

And what was the very first joke that the little white mouse told the lion?

Why – that he had one hundred and twenty-seven aunts and uncles and brothers and sisters, and that they were ALL coming to share the lion's big beautiful cave. And do you know what?

The lion didn't mind one bit.

"No one minds sharing in this house," says Little Ghost. "There are lots of people who live here."

"Very true," agrees Big Ghost, "very true."

"And I'm here too," Little Ghost says, and he giggles. "They don't know about us, do they?"

Big Ghost shakes his head. "I don't think they do."

"See you next week, then," Little Ghost says.

"See you next week," says Big Ghost.

# WEEK 40

*It's a cold stormy evening. Big Ghost is in the kitchen, and Little Ghost is glad to sit on the top of a radiator and warm up.*

*"B'rrrr!" he says. "It's wet out there!"*

*"It certainly is," says Big Ghost. "Daisy B fell in a puddle, and she had to have all her clothes washed!"*

*"I was thinking about Daisy B," says Little Ghost. "I was thinking that you haven't told me a Daisy B story for ages. "*

## Daisy B's Potty

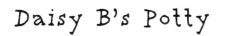

Mum wants Daisy B to sit on her potty.

Daisy B says "No!"

Julius says, "Wouldn't it be much nicer not to wear nappies?"

Daisy B says, "Yes!"

Daisy B pulls off her nappy.

Mum says, "Good girl, Daisy B. Now, come and sit on your potty."

Daisy B says, "No!"

Julius says, "Will you sit on your potty if I bring you a drink?"

Daisy B says, "Yes!"

OOOOOPS!!!

"Oh, Daisy B!" says Julius. "Couldn't you have waited?"

Daisy B says, "No!"

Mum says, "Never mind."

Mum says, "Tim – please fetch Daisy B a new nappy."

Tim comes with the new nappy.

"Huh! Daisy B's a real baby," Tim says. "She'll wear nappies for ever and ever and ever."

"NO!" says Daisy B, and she sits right down on her potty.

OOOOOOOH!!!

Daisy B smiles.

"OH! Daisy B!" say Mum and Julius and Tim. "You are so clever!"

"Yes!" said Daisy B.

"She's not a baby now, is she?" asks Little Ghost. "She's a little girl."

"Yes," says Big Ghost. "And you're not a baby either – but I think maybe you'd better be getting home before this weather gets any worse. "

# WEEK 41

*It's a cold crisp night, and Big Ghost is swinging on the washing line when Little Ghost arrives.*

*"Can I do that too?" he asks.*

*"If we sit in the peg bag," says Big Ghost, "we can have our story out here."*

*"Can it be about the butterfies and snails again?" says Little Ghost.*

*"Just what I was about to suggest," says Big Ghost.*

## Mary Moth to the Rescue

One spring evening Clive Caterpillar was sitting on a stinging nettle and chatting with his friends.

"When I'm a butterfly," Clive said, "I shall fly higher than any butterfly has ever flown before."

"Oooooh!" Susie Slug went pale. She was frightened of heights.

"Oh, Clive!" said Mary Moth. "You'll get very dizzy!"

"Not me," boasted Clive. "I shall fly up and up until I can see the top of the clouds."

"Height isn't everything," said Stuart Snail. "I can't fly, but last week I slithered all the way from one end of the garden to the other."

"Yes, but it took you four days," said Clive. "When I'm a butterfly I shall fly from one end of the garden to the other in two minutes."

"Oh, Clive!" said Mary Moth. "You'll get very tired!"

"No I won't," said Clive. "In fact, I shall probably fly all the way round the world and back by dinnertime."

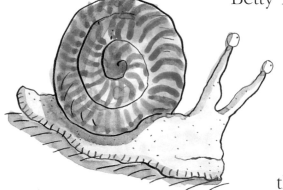

Betty Butterfly came fluttering by and stopped to listen.

"What are you going to do by dinnertime, Clive?" she asked.

Clive blushed bright pink.

"Nothing," he said.

"He says he's going to fly all the way round the world and back by dinnertime," said Stuart.

"He'll get very tired, won't he, Betty?" Mary asked.

Betty gave Clive a cold hard stare. "Clive had better wait and see what sort of butterfly he is before he goes flying round the world," she said. "He might be a cabbage white."

Clive looked cross.

"And I might not be," he said.

"Could you fly all the way round the world, Betty?" Susie Slug asked.

"I expect I could if I wanted to," said Betty, and she stretched her wings.

"Ooooh!" Susie stared. "You're wonderful, Betty."

"Of course she couldn't," said Stuart. "Really! Sometimes I think you'd believe anything, Susie."

Betty quivered her antennae and frowned at Stuart. "It's a little too late to fly round the world tonight," she said, "but I could fly all the way to the big tree down by the stream and back."

"That's a very long way," Mary Moth said. "Wouldn't it be better to do it tomorrow?"

"When I'm a butterfly – " Clive began.

"Be quiet, Clive," said Stuart. "Let's see if Betty can fly to the big tree and back."

"But it's getting dark," Mary said anxiously.

Betty fluttered her wings. "I'll be back before the stars come out," she said. "Don't you worry about me, Mary Moth." And off she flew into the twilight.

Susie, Stuart, Mary and Clive sat and waited.

And waited.

And waited.

The twilight faded away, and stars began to twinkle in the dark blue night sky.

"She's not back yet," said Susie in a very small voice. "Do you think she's all right, Stuart?"

Stuart was feeling guilty. He knew Betty would never have gone on such a long journey if he hadn't suggested it, but he wasn't going to tell anyone how how he was feeling. He snapped at Susie instead.

"Don't fuss, Susie. Didn't she say she could fly round the world? A butterfly who can do that will think nothing of a little trip down to the tree and back."

"That's right," said Clive, but he didn't sound very sure.

"Maybe I should go and have a look," said Mary Moth.

"YOU?" said Clive rudely. "What could you do?"

"Well … moths can see in the dark," Mary said. "I'll just see if I can see her anywhere, and then I'll come back again." And she fluttered off into the darkness.

"Oh dear," said Susie, and a silver tear slid down her nose.

"Perhaps Betty's gone for ever! And now Mary will disappear too. Oh dear oh dear oh dear!"

"I think you and Clive should go home to bed," said Stuart. "There's no point in all of us waiting around here doing nothing."

"Oh, but I couldn't sleep," said Susie. "I'd be much too worried about Betty and Mary to even close my eyes!"

"I can close my eyes," Clive said, and he wriggled away under the leaves.

Mary Moth flew steadily down the garden towards the big tree. As she flew she listened to all the night noises of the garden, but she could hear nothing out of the ordinary until –

"Help!"

It was the faintest of cries, but Mary turned and headed towards the rose bushes. She was almost sure that the voice had come from there … and as she flew nearer it came again.

"Help!"

"That's Betty!" thought Mary, and she called, "Where are you, Betty? I'm coming!"

There was a butterfly-sized sniff from in among the roses.

"I seem to have flown into a spider's web," Betty said miserably. "Do be careful, Mary! It's very big!"

Mary could see Betty now. She was stuck fast in the middle of a large and tattered web strung between two rose bushes, and she looked very unhappy. Mary flew down to have a better look, being careful not to get too near.

"H'm," said Mary as she inspected the web, "I think we need Stuart."

"Stuart?" Betty feebly waggled her antennae. "Oh, don't tell Stuart, Mary. He'll laugh at me, and tell me how silly I am."

"I'm sure he won't," Mary said in her most comforting voice.

"Oh he will!" Betty wailed. "And the worst of it is that he'll be quite right!"

Mary didn't answer. She was trying to work out a plan to rescue Betty. A tall garden fork was stuck in the ground a little way away, and Mary was wondering if it would break through the web if she pushed it over … but how could a very small moth move a human's garden fork? Her plan for Stuart was much simpler. If Stuart climbed up one of the bushes and fell into the spider's web he would break it easily.

"No," Mary said at last. "I'm sorry, Betty, but we really do need Stuart."

"I'm here!" said a voice from down below on the ground.

Mary was so shocked that she flew straight into the web.

"Oh no!" gasped Betty. "Mary! How could you?"

Down below Stuart coughed. He had seen what had happened. "Sorry. Didn't mean to frighten you. Er – what can I do to help?"

Mary lay very still. She knew that wriggling would only make the web stick more tightly.

Ooo dear, they're stuck!

"Stuart," she said, "you must climb up one of the rose bushes as high as you can – and then you must jump into the web. That'll break it – and Betty and I will be free."

"JUMP?" Stuart could hardly believe his ears. "Me? A snail? Jump?"

"Well – fall, then," said Mary. "Please Stuart. It's the best way."

Stuart slimed slowly towards the taller of the two rose bushes. He was not a happy snail. First of all it had been his fault that Betty had rushed off into the darkness, and now he'd made Mary fly into the web. "I only wanted to surprise her," he muttered to himself. "Super Snail, coming to the rescue. And what happens? It all goes wrong. And now they want me to jump. I wish I'd never got out of bed this morning."

Mary and Betty waited as patiently as they could as Stuart climbed up and up the rose bush. For a snail he was going fast; to Betty and Mary he seemed to be going terribly terribly slowly.

"Up," he panted. "That's the thing. Up! And up again!"

Higher and higher he climbed, until the branches at the top of the rose bush bent under his weight and the web trembled and shook.

"Oh no!" moaned Betty. "Is that the spider coming?"

"No," said Mary. "It's Stuart. He's nearly at the top. He'll be jumping any minute now. You'll soon be free, Betty."

Stuart clung to the very topmost branch of the rose bush. He was meaning to jump. He knew he had to, to save Betty and Mary. It was just that the branch would keep swaying to and fro –

"Ooooooh!" said Stuart. "I feel sick!" And he shut his eyes.

"It's all right, Stuart," said a tiny voice. "I'll jump with you. We'll jump together."

Stuart opened his eyes wide.

It was Susie Slug, right beside him, and she looked as cool as a cucumber.

"Ready?" asked Susie. "One – two – three – JUMP!"

Half way down to the web Stuart suddenly wondered if he really had jumped, or if Susie had given him a push. He didn't have time to decide, however, because just at that moment the two of them landed in the web –

and the web broke –

and Betty and Mary fluttered free.

All the way home Betty and Mary told Stuart and Susie how wonderful they were, and Susie glowed with pride. Stuart was rather strangely silent.

"Stuart the Super Snail," said Betty.

"Susie the Super Slug," said Mary.

"But I only followed Stuart because I was frightened of being left on my own," Susie said.

"But you jumped!" said Betty.

"You were amazing!" said Mary.

Stuart suddenly stopped. "I've just worked something out," he said.

"What's that, Stuart?" asked Betty.

"Well – if Mary hadn't come to find you you wouldn't be here now," said Stuart. "So we should thank Mary too."

"Mary Moth to the rescue!" said Susie.

"It was nothing," said Mary, and she blushed.

Stuart was about to say that it wasn't nothing when he was interrupted.

A sleepy voice from the nearby leaves said, "When I'M a butterfly I shall fly all the way up to the moon and back … and nobody will EVER need to rescue ME!"

*"Thank you, Big Ghost," says Little Ghost. "I like stories like that."*

*"Good," says Big Ghost, and Little Ghost squeezes out of the peg bag and floats away home.*

# WEEK 42

*Little Ghost arrives early tonight. He finds Big Ghost asleep on top of his cupboard.*

*"Big Ghost!" Little Ghost says, "I can't wait any longer! PLEASE will you tell me some more about the kitten with no name? What did the cuckoo do?" Big Ghost rubs his eyes. "Oooooooh," he yawns. "Sit down, Little Ghost, and stop flapping about. You're making me chilly!"*

## The Kitten with no Name: Part Seven

The kitten woke up with a jump. He hadn't really meant to go to sleep. He'd just meant to have a little rest while the cuckoo found his mother, but he was very tired, and very hungry.

But where was the cuckoo? Surely he should have come back by now?

The kitten stared up into the sky, but all he could see were white fluffy clouds.

"Cuckoo! Cuckoo! Cuckoo!" The kitten jumped again. There was a loud flapping of wings, and the cuckoo landed beside him with a thump.

"Coo! Did you see that landing!" The cuckoo was looking very pleased with himself.

"Yes," said the kitten. "It was very clever. It was very clever indeed … excuse me, but did you see my mother?"

"What?" The cuckoo tweaked a tail feather into place. "Oh, yes. She's not far away. She was sitting on a wall in front of a house, a big place. Thought you said you lived in a hedge?"

The kitten was breathless with excitement. "You saw her? Are you sure it was my mother? Did you tell her I was coming? Did you say I was here?"

"One thing at a time!" The cuckoo took a step backwards.

"Certainly looked like you. White paws."

"Oh – yes! Yes! That's my mother!" The kitten was trembling all over. "Did you talk to her?"

"Didn't like to go bothering her," said the cuckoo. "She was being stroked by one of those humans – but we can be there in no time at all! Come on! It'll only take ten minutes to get there. Follow me!" And the cuckoo began to get ready for take off.

"Wait!" The kitten scrambled after the cuckoo. "How will I follow you? I can't fly!"

"Listen, little four paws – you're talking to the best flyer in the field!" the cuckoo said cheerfully. "I can fly fast, and I can fly slow.

I can fly forwards, and I can fly backwards. Just keep your little peepers open, and shout if you get left behind."

"Oh! Oh!" The kitten could hardly speak. "Oh, thank you – thank you so much! Can we go now? Can we go this minute?"

"Certainly can," said the cuckoo, and with a swoop and a swerve and a dip and a dive he was up in the air above the kitten's head. "Cuckoo! Here we go!"

It was a good deal longer than ten minutes before the kitten struggled out of the long grass. He was worn out, and so hungry that his tummy was hurting. The thistles in the field hurt his paws, and prickly burrs clung to his soft fur, and the grass was so long that he had to push his way through. The cuckoo flew above him shouting "Not far to go now!" and "Keep going, little four paws!", but it was a long hard journey. When he finally struggled out and saw a wooden fence in front of him he gave a faint "Mew!" and collapsed in a heap.

"Cuckoo!" called the cuckoo. "Little four paws! Don't give up now!"

The kitten looked up. "I want my mother!" he said, and two huge tears rolled down his nose.

"Don't cry, little four paws – don't cry!" said the cuckoo, and he flew over the fence and round to the steps by the big house front door. Two children were making a fuss of a big stripy cat with white paws, and the cat was purring loudly.

"Cuckoo!" shouted the cuckoo at the top of his voice. "Cuckoo! Cuckoo! Cuckoo!"

The kitten tried to heave himself back up onto his feet. His legs wobbled badly, but he took a few staggering steps.

"Mew!" he said feebly. "Mew!"

"Poor little thing!" said a voice, and the kitten was scooped up and cuddled. He struggled for a moment, and then shut his eyes. It was warm and comfortable … but where was his mother?

"Put him in the basket," said another voice. "Fat Freda'll look after him."

The kitten felt himself carried along and up some steps, but his eyes were much too tired to open and see where he was going. He was gently put down somewhere very soft …

… and then he heard the most wonderful sound in the whole wide world.

He heard purring, and the purring was coming closer.

And closer.

And closer.

"Mother!" whispered the kitten.

And as a long pink tongue began to lick him clean he gave a little happy sigh and went to sleep.

*"Is that the end?" whispers Little Ghost.*

*Big Ghost is just about to answer when Little Ghost interrupts him.*

*"I know what you're going to say. You're going to say, 'wait and see!' " says Little Ghost. "Aren't you?"*

*Big Ghost nods.*

*Little Ghost is thinking so hard that he's frowning. "But Fat Freda isn't his mummy. Her kittens all had names, and they're grown up now."*

*Big Ghost nods again.*

*Little Ghost gives up. "I'll have to wait and see, won't I?"*

Let's go to page 246 for the last part of kitten's story.

Cool!

# WEEK 43

*Big Ghost and Little Ghost are very comfortable tonight. They're tucked up in the airing cupboard on the top landing, and Little Ghost is waiting for his story.*

*"Oh! I forgot to tell you! I heard something rustling when I was on my way here," Little Ghost says. "There's something squeaky in that room halfway up the stairs. Do you know what it is?"*

*Big Ghost laughs. "That's Ross's pet rat," he says. "And that reminds me of a story."*

## Why Rats are Never Pink or Purple

Long long ago, when there were king rats and queen rats and prince rats and princess rats, there was a rat called Princess Ratima who wanted to be different.

"I don't want to be brown," she said. "And I don't like my scaly tail. And I don't like my big yellow teeth."

She moaned and she groaned. She fussed and she bothered. She whinged and she whined so much that at last the other rats began to think she must be right.

"We don't like being brown either," they said. "And we don't like our scaly tails. And we hate our big yellow teeth!"

And they moaned and they groaned. And they fussed and they bothered. And they whinged and they whined so much that the wise old owl who lived in the tallest oak tree said, "Stop moaning! If you don't like the way you are, then change it!"

"Oh!" said the rats. "What a wise old owl! That's just what we'll do – we'll change the way we are!"

"But I like the way we are," said a very small voice.

All the other rats turned to stare. "Who said that?" they asked.

"It was me," said the very small voice, and a very small rat came out from a very small hole.

"Oh," said Princess Rat. "It's only Rattie."

The other rats sniggered. Rattie was the very smallest rat of all, and he didn't know anything about anything.

"Come on," said Princess Ratima. "Let's go. You can stay here, Rattie."

But Rattie went too. He didn't want to be left behind all on his own.

The rats went up the hills and down the hills and up the tallest hill of all – all the way to the very top where the big blue wizard lived in his big blue house.

"Please, Big Blue Wizard," said Princess Ratima. "Please will you make us different?"

"I might," said Big Blue Wizard. "Or then again, I might not. What will you do for me? A fair exchange is a fair exchange."

The rats scratched their ears. They couldn't think of anything. Then Rattie had an idea.

"We could polish your windows," he said. "We could sweep your floors. We could shine your shoes."

"That sounds like a fair offer," said Big Blue Wizard. "If you do that for seven days I'll give you one wish each."

Princess Ratima and the rats were very excited. They hurried into the big blue house, and for seven days they polished windows. For seven days they swept the floors. For seven days they shined Big Blue Wizard's collection of big blue shoes. At last there was nothing left to do.

"Good," said Big Blue Wizard. "Very good. You may have one wish each, but be careful. Wishes don't always bring happiness."

The rats didn't listen. They had already started wishing, and KERBOOM!

Suddenly the big blue house was full of brightly coloured rats. There were green rats with furry tails. There were blue rats with curly tails. There were yellow rats with hairy tails. Princess Ratima was pink with a fluffy tail – and every single rat had neat little white teeth and big big smiles.

Only Rattie stayed the same. He was still a small brown rat with a scaly tail and long yellow teeth.

"Hey, little rat!" said Big Blue Wizard. "What about your wish?"

Rattie shook his head. "I'm quite happy as I am," he said. "But thank you for asking." He sighed heavily. "But I don't look like the other rats any more. Can I stay here with you when they all go home?"

"I'd be glad of the company," said Big Blue Wizard. "But any time you want your wish, just ask."

At first the rainbow rats were very happy. They scampered down the tallest hill dancing and singing. They told each other how lovely they were, and they took turns brushing their tails. Princess Fatima said that she was the happiest rat in all the land.

But soon things began to go wrong. The fluffy, furry, curly, hairy tails dragged in the mud and the dirt. The rats couldn't gnaw and chew with their little white teeth. Worst of all, they could never ever hide away. All the other animals could see them, and the cats chased them high and low and round and about all day and every day.

"I'm hungry," said Princess Ratima. "And I'm tired of being chased."

"We're hungry too," said the other rats. "And we're very tired of being chased. We want to be the way we were!"

So they trooped back up the hills and down the hils and up the tallest hill of all to see the big blue wizard.

"Well well well," said Big Blue Wizard. "Back so soon?"

"Please may we go back to being the way we were?" begged the rats. "We'll clean your windows and sweep your floor and shine your shoes for as long as you like!"

"No," said Big Blue Wizard. "One wish only. That's the rule, and rules is rules." And he was just about to shut the door when Rattie hopped onto his big blue foot.

"Excuse me," he said, "but do I still have a wish?"

"You certainly do," said Big Blue Wizard.

"Then can I wish the rats to be the way they were?" asked Rattie.

"Waste of a wish, if you ask me," said Big Blue Wizard.

Rattie shook his head. "It's very lonely being the only brown rat in the whole wide world," he said.

"Well," said Big Blue Wizard. "It's your wish."

"Then that's what I wish," said Rattie, and KERBOOOOOOM!!!!!

All the rats were brown with scaly tails and long yellow teeth …

well, nearly all.

There were one or two black rats. And one or two white rats. And a scattering of piebald rats and spotty rats and brown and white rats. But they all had scaly tails, and they all had long yellow teeth.

And so it always has been, and always will be, and very very beautiful they are too.

Oh, did I mention that Princess Ratima married Rattie? And she became a much nicer rat, and they lived happily ever after.

*"Is that the rat in Ross's room?" asks Little Ghost.*

*"It might be one of his relations," says Big Ghost.*

*"I'll have a tiny peep at him on my way out," Little Ghost says, and he tiptoes away down the stairs.*

# WEEK 44

WHOOOOSH!!!! Little Ghost falls down the kitchen chimney in such a hurry that Fat Freda leaps up with all her fur standing on end.

"Sorry," says Little Ghost. "But I'm fed up. First of all Mama Ghost kept on talking to her friends, and now she wants me to go home early."

"Never mind," says Big Ghost. "We've still got time for a tiny story."

## Spin! Spin! Spin!

When I spin my web I go round and round and round and round and round and round and round and round and round … and I say to the flies "Do come in and see me spin! Let me show you how I twist my thread that way – do come a little closer! – and I throw a line that way – do step a little nearer ! – and I dance over my web up and up and down and round and round and … oh, Mr Fly – did you fall in?

"Poor old Mr Fly," says Little Ghost, but before he can say anything else there's a WHOOOOOO!!! down the chimney.

"Ooops," says Little Ghost. "I've got to go!"

And Big Ghost just has time to nod before Little Ghost disappears again …

# WEEK 45

*The dog basket is full tonight, but not with dogs. Big Ghost is in there, and so is Little Ghost.*

*"We have to have a dog story if we're in here," says Little Ghost. "Please, Big Ghost – tell me about the other dog. Not Hunter – I know about him. Tell me about the little one."*

## Tiny and the kittens

A long time ago a puppy came to live in this house. His name was Tiny, but he didn't know who had chosen his name. He didn't remember his mother. He didn't remember his father. All he knew was that he lived in a big house and there was a warm cosy basket in the kitchen, and a big fat cat to keep him company.

Fat Freda looked after Tiny. She licked him clean and showed him how to lap milk from a bowl.

"Are you my mother?" Tiny asked.

"Meeow," said Fat Freda. "I'm a cat." And she licked his ear.

One day there were four little kittens in the basket as well as Tiny and Fat Freda. Fat Freda licked the kittens clean, and she went on looking after Tiny too.

"Are they my brothers and sisters?" Tiny asked.

"Meeow," said Fat Freda. "They're little kitties." And she licked his nose.

The kittens grew and grew. At first they stayed in the basket with their eyes tightly shut, but when their eyes opened they began to stagger around on little wobbly legs. Tiny watched them anxiously, but Fat Freda didn't worry. If they went too far she picked them up by the scruff of their necks and popped them back in their basket.

"Meeow," she said. "Such little dears!"

Soon the kittens were jumping and bouncing all over the kitchen. They pulled Tiny's ears, and they swung on his tail.

"Ow!" said Tiny. "Don't do that!"

The kittens took no notice.

Tiny went to complain to Fat Freda.

"Meeow," said Fat Freda. "They're only little."

The kittens grew bigger still. They climbed on Tiny's back, and sometimes they scratched his nose with their sharp little claws.

"Ow!" said Tiny. "Don't do that!"

The kittens took no notice.

Tiny got out of the basket and went to sit on the mat in front of the fire.

The kittens came too, and played hide and seek in between his legs.

"Meeow," said Fat Freda. "Aren't they pretty?"

Fat Freda showed the kittens how to lap milk out of a bowl. They drank their milk, and then they drank Tiny's milk.

"Woof!" said Tiny.

"Meeow," said Fat Freda. "Aren't they growing into fine little cats?"

Fat Freda taught the kittens to eat kitty crunchies and kitty dinners. Tiny gobbled his dinner very fast, just in case the kittens tried to eat his dinner as well as theirs.

"Meeow," said Fat Freda. "Eat nicely, Tiny dear."

Two days later Tiny woke up late. He yawned, stretched, and went to find his breakfast – and there were the four little kittens, licking the very bottom of his bowl.

"WOOF!" Tiny barked so loudly that the kittens jumped. "WOOF! I WANT MY BREAKFAST!" And he growled for the very first time in his life. The kittens froze, their fur standing up on end until they looked like puffballs.

"GRRRRRRR!!!!" Tiny chased the kittens round and round the kitchen, out through the cat flap, and down the garden path. Off and away they rushed, in and out of the bushes, twice round the garden pond, past the garden shed and –

scramble scramble scritch scratch scritch!

The four little kittens scrambled their way up the apple tree and up onto a long branch. "Meeeeeeeow! Meeeeeeeow! Meeeeeeeeow!" they wailed. "Mother! Mother! Mother!"

"THERE!" shouted Tiny. "Maybe that'll teach you a lesson! I'm tired of having my ears pulled! And my tail swung on! And my nose scratched! And my milk drunk! And don't you ever EVER eat my breakfast again!"

And Tiny stomped back into the house, leaving the kittens up in the tree.

It was very quiet in the kitchen.

Tiny sat down in the basket, and stretched.

"Aaaaah," he sighed. "Room at last. How lovely."

But he couldn't go to sleep. Somehow the basket felt too big, and too empty.

Tiny went to sit on the mat.

That felt wrong too.

There was no one to snuggle up to. There was no one to play with. There was no one to lick his nose and purr.

Tiny scratched his ears and tried to work out what was wrong.

"I feel odd because I'm hungry," he decided.

He went to look in his bowl. It was still empty, but he saw that the kittens' bowl was full.

"I could eat their breakfast!" he thought. "After all, they ate mine!"

He ate two crunchies, and then stopped. He wasn't hungry any more.

"OH!" said Tiny. "I'm LONELY!"

Do you think Tiny is lonely?

Tiny went rushing back out of the cat flap.

The kittens were still on their branch. Fat Freda was sitting underneath the tree washing her paws.

"Meeow," she said. "What silly little kitties. They climbed the tree, and now they can't get down!"

Tiny hung his head. "They didn't climb the tree, Fat Freda," he said. "I chased them up there."

Fat Freda began to wash her tail. "Did you, dear?" she said.

Tiny looked at Fat Freda. Then he looked up at the four little kittens.

"Woof!" he said. "Please come down!"

The four little kittens shook their heads.

"I won't chase you any more," said Tiny.

The kittens shook their heads again.

"You can pull my ears," said Tiny. "Just as long as it's not too hard. And I won't mind if you swing on my tail sometimes. And you can climb on my back."

The kittens still shook their heads.

Tiny took a deep breath. "All right," he said. "I promise not to growl and chase you – just as long as you promise **not** to eat all my breakfast. We can share – "

PLOP! PLOP! PLOP! PLOP!

Four little kittens jumped out of the tree. They bounced round Tiny and pulled his ears – but not too hard. They swung on his tail – and then they stopped. They climbed on his back, and Tiny carried them carefully along the path and up to the cat flap, and then they curled up together in the basket – after Tiny had eaten all the kitty crunchies.

"Meeow," said Fat Freda.

*Little Ghost is so pleased that he does twirly whirlies all the way round and round the room.*

*"I know those kittens!" he says. "One of them is Big Tom, and he still lives here! And the others are the girl kittens!" He stops whirling for a moment. "Do any of them live here?"*

*"Kitty Purr," says Big Ghost. "She's Granny Annie's cat."*

*"Oh," says Little Ghost. "I haven't seen her about much."*

*"She comes and goes," says Big Ghost, "she comes and goes."*

*"Like me!" says Little Ghost. "I came for my story – and now I'm going! Goodbye, Big Ghost!"*

# WEEK 46

*Big Ghost is in the playroom tonight, and Little Ghost finds him dozing inside the Noah's Ark.*

*"It doesn't look very comfortable in there," he says.*

*"It is a bit knobbly," Big Ghost agrees, and he floats out and onto the rug.*

*"You were asleep on top of the elephant," says Little Ghost.*

*"So I was," says Big Ghost. "It was to remind me to tell you an elephant story."*

This is a good story!

## The Elephant who had no Friends

The lion and the cheetah and the monkey and the elephant were friends. They played together, and they visited each other, and they often had swimming parties in the great blue lake, but one day they had an argument.

"I'm the best in all the jungle!" said the lion. "I've got the biggest roar!" and he roared a terrible roar to prove it.

"That's nothing," said the cheetah. "That's just a lot of noise. I can run – and I can run faster than any of you, so I'm the best!" and he ran all the way round the great blue lake and back again in no time at all. "There!" he said. "Told you I was best!"

"I don't know why you think running is so special," said the monkey.

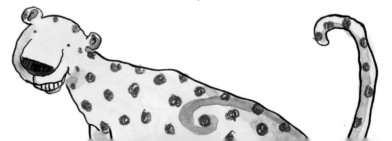

"I can swing through the trees, and I can climb to the top of the palm tree any time I want a banana. Watch!" and he swung in and out of the creepers and up the tallest palm tree. "Who's the best now?" he said, and he dropped a bunch of bananas THUNK!!! in front of the elephant.

"Roaring and running and swinging and climbing are all very well, my friends," said the elephant, "but the most important thing of all is strength. I'm afraid you're all wrong. It's me that's the best in the jungle – because I'm the strongest!"

And the elephant picked up the lion and threw him in the great blue lake. *SPLASH!!!!*

Then he threw the cheetah after the lion. *SPLASH!!!!*

Then he threw the monkey after the cheetah. *SPLASH!!!!*

"See?" said the elephant. "I'm the best." And he helped himself to a banana.

The lion and the cheetah and the monkey dragged themselves out of the water.

"That was a horrible thing to do," said the lion.

"You're mean," said the cheetah.

"And you're greedy too," said the monkey. "Those were my bananas. I don't want to be friends with you any more."

"Nor me," said the cheetah.

"Go away and leave us alone," said the lion.

The lion, the cheetah and the monkey went off together, and the elephant was left standing in the middle of his banana skins.

"Oh dear," he said to himself. "Perhaps I shouldn't have done that. Still – I expect we'll all be friends again soon."

The elephant was wrong. The lion and the cheetah and the monkey wouldn't talk to him. They wouldn't listen when he tried to say sorry. They said "Go away!" when he asked them to play hide and seek. They didn't want to be friends with a greedy show-off elephant who threw them in the great blue lake.

The elephant grew lonely. There was no one to talk to, and no one to play with. He wandered through the long grass and felt sorry for himself.

"Maybe I'll go down to the great blue lake," he said, "and have a bath. There's nothing else to do." He sighed heavily. "I expect the lion and the cheetah and the monkey will be somewhere having fun without me. Oh, I do wish they'd be my friends again!"

The elephant walked slowly and sadly down through the grass to the great blue lake. As he came nearer he could hear the lion roaring with laughter, and the cheetah cackling, and the monkey giggling. The elephant peered through the trees.

"Just as I thought," he said. "They're having fun. They don't miss me at all." A tear trickled down his trunk. "I think I'll go back home. I don't feel like a bath any more." And he was just about to turn

round and trudge away when he stopped. Something had caught his eye, and it wasn't the lion diving from a rock, or the cheetah showing off his back stroke, or the monkey splashing in the shallow water.

The elephant screwed up his eyes and looked again. Yes! Something was moving. Something was creeping slowly … slowly … slowly along the edge of the great blue lake. Something was creeping slowly … slowly …. slowly nearer and nearer to the monkey. Something was slowly … slowly … slowly opening its huge wide mouth full of long sharp teeth …

The elephant charged out of the trees. "TRUMPETTY TRUMPETTY TRUMPETTY!" he yelled, and he scooped up the crocodile and he threw it right into the very middle of the great blue lake.

The lion and the cheetah and the monkey stared, and then they swam and sploshed and paddled towards the elephant as fast as they could go.

"Hurrah for you!" they shouted. "You're the best friend ever!"

The elephant smiled a happy smile. "Thank you," he said, and then he coughed a small awkward cough. "Ahem. I'm very sorry I threw you all in the great blue lake. I promise I won't do it again."

"And I won't boast about having the best roar ever," said the lion.

"And I won't show off my super speedy running," said the cheetah.

"Why don't I climb up a palm tree and fetch us all some bananas?" said the monkey. "Then we can have a party!"

"A best friends party?" said the elephant hopefully.

"YES!" said the lion and the cheetah and the monkey, and they did.

*"That's a nice ending," says Little Ghost. "I'm glad they made friends again. We're friends, aren't we, Big Ghost?"*

*"We certainly are," says Big Ghost. "I'd miss you if you didn't come every week."*

*"I'd miss you too," says Little Ghost. "See you next week!"*

# WEEK 47

*Little Ghost is looking puzzled as he drifts into the sitting room through the open window.*

*"What's the matter, Little Ghost?" asks Big Ghost.*

*"I was just wondering," says Little Ghost. "I was just wondering if Ross and Tia and Tim and Jason and Daisy B have ever seen a ghost like me."*

*"I'm not sure about Daisy B," says Big Ghost, "but there was a baby ghost who came to visit here once."*

### Woooo! Wooooo!

There was once an old old castle on the edge of a wood. In the old old castle was an old old tower, and in the old old tower was an old old room. In the old old room was an old old chimney, and in the old old chimney lived three ghosts.

There were two great big ghosts and one very little one, and every evening they went out haunting. They wailed and they moaned and they moaned and they wailed – but as no one ever came to the old old castle there was no one to see them and be scared. Papa Ghost didn't mind, and Mama Ghost didn't mind – but Baby Ghost was bored.

"Can't we move?" he asked. "Couldn't we move to the village at the bottom of the hill? I want to be able to scare real people. I want to go *Woooo! Woooo! Woooo!* and make them run away."

"But we've always lived here," said Papa Ghost.

"That's right," said Mama Ghost. "This is our home."

"Well," said Baby Ghost, "I'll go and do some scaring on my own. I'll be back later." And he twirled twice round the chimney pot and flew away over the hill and down to the village.

The village seemed very noisy to Baby Ghost. There were cars hooting and buses tooting, bells ringing and doors slamming, and lots of people rushing up and down the pavements.

Baby Ghost floated this way and that looking at it all.

"There are certainly lots of people here," he said to himself. "But how will they hear me go *Woooo! Woooo?*"

He slipped through an open window and found himself in a big shop. It was busy, but it was quieter than the road outside.

"*Woooo! Woooo! Woooo!*" wailed Baby Ghost happily, and he waved his little white arms. "*Woooo! Woooo! Woooo!*"

Nobody took any notice.

"Bother!" said Baby Ghost. He twirled up and down a staircase.

"*Woooo! Woooo! Woooo!*" he called. "*Woooo! Woooo! Woooo!*"

"Fancy!" said a woman with a shopping basket. "There's something that looks like a ghost! What will they think of next?"

Her friend stopped to look. "It doesn't look very real," she said, and she went off to look at hats.

Baby Ghost didn't understand it. "It's very odd," he said to himself. "Why aren't they frightened? Maybe I'd better try somewhere else." He floated out of the shop and into a tall thin house where two big boys were sitting watching televison. Baby Ghost swooped down with his very loudest "*Woooo!*" but they didn't even turn round.

Can you go Wooo! Wooo!

"Go away, Tiddles," said one boy. "It's too early for your kitty crunchies." He turned up the sound on the television.

"Silly cat," said the other boy.

"What's wrong with me?" Baby Ghost wondered as he slid silently away through a crack under the door. "Aren't I big enough? Aren't I scary enough?"

Outside the traffic was still rushing up and down the road. Baby Ghost sighed. "Maybe I should go home. I don't think I'm any good at scaring people after all." And he drooped against a lamp post.

"Hello," said a voice. "What are you doing here?"

Baby Ghost looked up.

Right in front of him was another little ghost, and she was smiling at him. "The party's down the road," she said.

"Party?" said Baby Ghost. "What party?"

"Jason's fancy dress party, of course," said the little ghost. "Come on, or we'll be late!" And she ran off.

"Why doesn't she fly?" thought Baby Ghost, but he hurried after her all the same.

The party had already started when Baby Ghost and the little girl ghost arrived. Baby Ghost stared around him in wonder. He had never seen so many strange-looking creatures. There were cats and bears and monsters and witches … and there, jumping up and down, was another little ghost.

"I'm a ghost!" he shouted. "*Woooo! Wooooo!*"

Two little monsters screamed. "Ooooh!

Wooo! Wooo!!

Jason, you're so scary!"

Baby Ghost cheered up at once.

"*Woooo! Woooo!*" he wailed, and the monsters screamed again, even louder.

Just then Jason's big brother Ross came into the room.

"Mum says you've got time for a game before tea," he said. "What shall we play?"

"Hide and seek!" yelled Jason. "Everyone hide!"

"I'll be the finder!" said Ross. "I'll count to ten and then find you!"

Baby Ghost had never played hide and seek before, but he thought it was fun – even though Ross found him almost at once.

"You've got glowing stuff on your costume," Ross said. "You shine in the dark. Come and help me find the others!"

They found the other children hidden behind curtains, in cupboards, under the bed, crouching behind chairs, but when Mum came to call them for tea there was still someone missing.

Baby Ghost couldn't find Jason.

Nor could Ross.

"Where's Jason?" he asked, but nobody knew.

"Maybe he's in the garden?" said Ross, and
everybody tumbled out of the kitchen door –
everybody except Baby Ghost. He wasn't quite
sure, but he thought he'd heard a giggle. He
slipped silently back into the hall and floated
up the stairs.

There was no giggle at the top of the
stairs, but Baby Ghost could hear another
noise.

Someone was crying, and rattling at a door.

Baby Ghost looked round, and saw a
cupboard.

"Hello!" he called. "Are you in there?"

The crying stopped suddenly.

"I wasn't crying," Jason said in a sniffly kind of voice through the keyhole.
"I was just making a noise because I'm stuck. I locked the door and I
dropped the key and now I can't find it because it's very very dark and
horrid in here and I don't much like it!" And he began to kick and rattle the
door loudly.

Baby Ghost looked at the keyhole. "Just my size," he said, and with a
twist and a wriggle he popped through.

"Hello!" he said.

Jason's eyes opened very wide in the darkness.

There was a faint glow all around Baby Ghost, and he was floating in the air.

"Oh!" Jason whispered. "You're a real ghost!"

Baby Ghost smiled proudly.

"Terrific!" breathed Jason. "I've always wanted to see a real ghost!"

Baby Ghost stared at Jason. "Aren't you real too?" he asked.

"Me?" Jason pulled the sheet off his head. "I'm a boy!"

"Oh!" said Baby Ghost. "I thought you were like me."

Jason shook his head. "I can't shine like you," he said. "Oh! I know! Can you shine yourself a bit lower? Yes – that's it! Look! I can see the key!" And Jason snatched the key off the floor and clicked it into the lock. The door opened, and Jason fell out with a loud shout of "Here I am!" just as Ross and the children came hurrying up the stairs.

Baby Ghost looked at them all for a moment, and he saw the monsters had taken their heads off. He saw the cats had smudged their whiskers, the bears had no ears, the witch had lost her teeth. They were all like Jason. None of them was real.

Baby Ghost slid away out of the window.

"Ross!" said Jason as he dusted himself down. "Ross! There's a real live ghost and I saw it! He's here at my party! He helped me get out of that horrid old cupboard!" He turned round to look for Baby Ghost …

but Baby Ghost wasn't there.

"Where is he?" asked Jason anxiously. "Ghost – ghost? Please don't go!"

"Come on, Jason," Ross said. "Mum's got tea ready." And Jason had to go down the stairs for his birthday tea.

Baby Ghost was hovering outside.

"I think I'll go home now," he said to himself. "I'm tired." He smiled. "But I'll come back here soon. I like this house. And I did make two monsters scream, so Poppa and Momma will be proud of me," and he floated off up the hill.

Ross was looking round the tea table in a puzzled way. The children were sitting at their places, and there were no empty chairs.

"What's the matter, Ross?" asked Mum.

"It's odd," Ross said. "When we were playing hide and seek there were three little ghosts. There was Jason, and Lucy, and another little one that glowed in the dark – and he's not here now, and there's no one missing."

Jason looked up from his sandwich. "See?" he said. "I told you there was a real ghost." He grinned at Ross. "*Wooooo! Wooooo! Wooooo!*"

Little Ghost looks at Big Ghost. "I don't know any old old castles," he says. "That Baby Ghost doesn't live near me." He sighs. "I wish he did. I could play with him."

"He'll come and play with you one day," says Big Ghost. "But he's very busy with his new little sister just now."

Little Ghost stares. "How do you know?" he asks.

Big Ghost laughs. "Because I'm his Grandfather Ghost!" he says, and he smiles at Little Ghost's astonished face. "That's how I heard all about what happened. Now, don't you think it's time you were going home?"

"Yes," says Little Ghost, and he goes slowly towards the window. "Will I really meet him one day?"

"If you want to," says Big Ghost.

"Oh, I do!" says little Ghost. "Goodnight, Big Ghost!"

# WEEK 48

*It's a quiet sunny evening. The kitten with no name is patting at a ball of fluff under the kitchen table when Little Ghost arrives, and Big Ghost is lying back on the hearth rug.*

*"Is Baby Ghost coming tonight?" Little Ghost wants to know.*

*"No," says Big Ghost. "But the kitten's here. Would you like to hear the end of his story?"*

*"Yes please," says Little Ghost.*

## The Kitten with no Name: Part Eight

The kitten with no name was warm and cosy and comfortable. He wasn't in the fields any more. He wasn't under a gorse bush. He wasn't in a rabbit burrow. He wasn't even under the hedge where he had lived with his mother since he was born. He was tucked up in a fluffy rug, and he could hear a steady purring from the other side of the basket.

"There's Mother," he thought sleepily, and he opened his eyes.

The big cat with white paws opened her eyes at exactly the same time.

"Good morning, my dear," she said. "Did you sleep well?"

The kitten's eyes opened wider and wider. For a moment he could say nothing at all.

It looked like his mother. Very, very like his mother. The white paws were the same. Even the purr was the same kind of friendly growl.

It wasn't his mother.

The kitten sat up, his heart thumping . "Meeow!" he said. "Who are you? Where am I? Where's my mother?"

Fat Freda didn't answer. She gently lifted the kitten out of the basket and dropped him down beside a saucer of bread and milk. "Breakfast," she said.

The kitten paused for a moment, but the smell of the bread and the milk was too much for him. He ate and he ate, and when he had eaten so much that he couldn't manage a single drop more he stopped and licked his whiskers.

"Mew," he said. "Where am I?"

Fat Freda was cleaning her paws, but she stopped to pat the top of his head. "P'rrrrr. You'll feel better now," she said. "Haven't you come to live here? I thought you were the new kitten."

The kitten sighed. "I'm lost," he said sadly.

"Lost?" Fat Freda said. "Why, you poor little thing."

"Yes," said the kitten, and he told Fat Freda how he had walked all the way from his house under the hedge, and how he was looking for his mother.

"I've been miles and miles and miles and miles," the kitten said. "The mouse and the frog and the rabbit and the cuckoo all tried to help me, but I don't think I'll ever find my mother again. And I'll never find my house under the hedge either."

Fat Freda stood up and stretched. "What did you say your mother looked like?"

"Just like me," said the kitten. He looked at Fat Freda. "And like you my mother's tail has a white tip too."

"Fancy that," said Fat Freda, and she settled down again in a patch of sunshine. "One of my kittens had a white tip to her tail."

"Oh, she's not a kitten," said the kitten. "She's my mother!"

Fat Freda yawned. "All my kittens are grown up now," she said. "You'll see Big Tom soon. He's one of my kittens. And Kitty Purr is another. She lives at the very top of the house with Granny Annie. Well, she used to, but she went away. Nobody's seen her – MEEOW!"

"What is it?" asked the kitten. Fat Freda was looking wide awake for the first time that morning.

"Never you mind," said Fat Freda. "You just curl up and have a rest. When the family come home from shopping they'll all come rushing in here, but you mustn't mind them. They don't do any harm."

"Oh," said the kitten. He looked at Fat Freda. "Are you going away?"

"Not very far," Fat Freda said. "I'll be back soon."

The kitten watched Fat Freda stroll out of the kitchen. It seemed very big and empty now he was on his own; even the basket didn't feel as warm and cosy as it had done. He hopped out, and looked round.

"Woof! Woof woof woof! Woof woof woof WOOF!"

"Yap! Yap yap yap YAP!"

The kitten froze. The barking was outside, but it was getting nearer. His fur stood up on end, and he gave a tiny hiss, and then hurled himself across the carpet as the back door opened and a huge monster dog and a smaller toothy dog came dashing in. A rush of children and grown-ups and parcels and packages and bags came after them.

The kitten leapt behind the squashy old sofa and flattened himself against the wall, and saw a little pink basket hanging on the radiator. Without stopping to think he dived inside, and lay there quaking with fright.

The noises in the kitchen gradually settled down. The two dogs flumped down in front of the fire, and the grown-ups pottered about clattering things and putting them on the table. The children chatted to each other, and laughed, and the kitten began to listen to what was going on.

"Is Granny Annie coming down for tea?" asked a voice.

"No, she's too sad," someone answered. "She walked down to the shops to see if anyone had seen Kitty Purr, but nobody had."

"Kitty Purr's been missing for ages now," said another voice. "I don't think she'll ever come back."

"I wish we could find Granny Annie a new cat," said a boy's voice. "It's a shame there weren't any kittens in the pet shop."

The kitten pricked up his ears, and – very carefully – he peeped out of the basket. He was almost sure that he had seen the boy before.

"Daisy B's got a pretty kitty," said a squeaky little voice. "Granny Annie can play with my kitty."

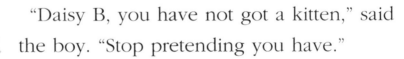

"Daisy B, you have not got a kitten," said the boy. "Stop pretending you have."

"Daisy B *has* got a kitty," said the little squeak.

The kitten's ears twitched. He remembered now. A long time ago the boy and the little girl had found him playing by his hedge, and the little girl had wanted to take him home.

Was this her house? The house where she lived? The tall boy had hugged him, and his mother had said that hugs were good. But what else had she said? The kitten's ears drooped. His mother had told him he must never ever go away with anyone, and here he was in the little girl's house. He sank down again in the little basket. What was going to happen to him? Whatever was he going to do?

He crouched down in the little pink basket.

"Kitty! There's my kitty!"

There was a loud clatter in the kitchen. Daisy B had got down from the table, and was running to the door.

"Daisy B!" said a grown-up. "You haven't finished your sandwich!"

"Heard my kitty," said Daisy B, and the kitten heard the back door open.

"Oh." Daisy B was nearly crying. "Isn't my kitty. Is *BIG* cats!"

There was a sudden silence. There was a meow, and then another. Fat Freda was calling to the kitten …

and another cat was calling too.

The kitten froze. Then he leapt out of the little pink basket –

"MOTHER!"

And this time it really was his mother, and she sprang towards him with a huge "Merrrup!" of joy, and licked him and purred over him and rolled him over and over with her paw until he was so dizzy that he didn't notice that all the people in the kitchen were laughing and cheering and clapping their hands.

Ross was shouting, "It's Kitty Purr! It's Kitty Purr! She's come back – somebody tell Granny Annie!"

Daisy B was shouting, "It's Daisy B's pretty kitty – he was in the basket!"

The kitchen door opened, and Granny Annie came hurrying in with a huge smile on her face.

"Kitty Purr!" she called. "Kitty Purr! Oh, wherever have you been?"

The kitten's mother ran to Granny Annie, and wound round and round her legs, purring loudly.

The kitten watched her go, and for a second he felt lonely. But then Daisy B picked him up. She hugged him and she hugged him, and it wasn't too tight. It was exactly the right sort of hug.

*"Prrrrr … prrrrr … " The kitten with no name is purring. Little Ghost is stroking him, and tickling his round fat tummy.*

*"So that's how he came to live here," says Little Ghost. "Kitty Purr is his mum, and Fat Freda is his granny!"*

*"Well done," says Big Ghost.*

*"But he still doesn't have a name," says Little Ghost. He pats the kitten's head, very gently. "Do you think he'll ever have one?"*

*"Keep your eyes and ears open, Little Ghost," says Big Ghost. "You never know – you might find his name for him!"*

*"Oh – I WILL!" Little Ghost promises.*

Do you want to know the kitten's name? I do.

# WEEK 49

*"Let's have a Daisy B story," Big Ghost says as Little Ghost slithers in through the keyhole. "She was having a bath tonight, and I remembered a story I know about her."*

## When Daisy B had a Bath

Daisy B is in the bath.
Daisy B fills up her little jug.
Daisy B pours water over her toes.
Mum says Clever Daisy B!
Daisy B fills up her little jug.
Daisy B pours water over her knees.
Mum says Clever Daisy B!
Dasiy B fills up her little jug.

Daisy B pours water over her head.

Mum says Clever Daisy B!

Daisy B smiles.

Daisy B is very clever.

Daisy B fills up her little jug.

Daisy B pours water over Mum's head.

*Little Ghost hoots with laughter. "What a funny girl," he says. "I'm glad the kitten with no name belongs to her."*

*Big Ghost stretches. "What story would you like next week, Little Ghost?"*

*"Please could we have a story about friends?" says Little Ghost.*

*"All right," says Big Ghost, "we'll have a story all about being friends."*

# WEEK 50

*Big Ghost is waiting for Little Ghost in the playroom.*

*"Would you like to choose an animal for your story?" he asks.*

*Little Ghost looks at the toys. "Can we have a leopard? OH! What's that?" And he points to a picture in an open book.*

*"That's a woodrat," says Big Ghost.*

## Bounding and Bouncing

Leopard and Woodrat were friends.

When Leopard bounded, Woodrat bounded.

When Woodrat bounced, Leopard bounced.

They played hide and seek

and catch as catch can

and Grandmother's Footsteps.

They played together every day.

Bear came prowling by on his way to hunt for honey. He stopped to watch Leopard finding Woodrat behind a flower.

"I know why you're friends," he said. "It's because you've both got tails."

"But my tail has a tuft on it," said Leopard.

"And my tail is long and thin," said Woodrat.

Frog jumped out of the water as Woodrat caught Leopard down by the pool.

"I know why you're friends," he said. "It's because you've both got whiskers."

"But my whiskers are long and wavy," said Leopard.

"And my whiskers are short and whiffly," said Woodrat.

Snake slid round a tree when Woodrat was tiptoeing up to Leopard.

"I know why you're friends." she said. "It's because you both have soft and silent feet."

"But my feet are big and pad pad paddy," said Leopard.

"And my feet are little and scritch scritch scritchy," said Woodrat.

"Maybe Leopard and Woodrat are friends because one of them is smooth and one of them is curly," said Snake.

"Maybe they're friends because one of them is big and one of them is little," said Frog.

"Maybe they're friends because one of them has a roar and the other has a squeak," said Bear.

Bear and Frog and Snake watched at Leopard and Woodrat playing hoppity skip and skippety hop.

"Why ARE you friends?" they all asked together.

Leopard and Woodrat looked at each other and began to laugh.

"We don't know!" said Woodrat.

"We just are!" said Leopard.

And Woodrat and Leopard gave each other a huge hug.

Then they looked at Bear and Frog and Snake.

"Why don't you come and play tomorrow?" they asked.

"Can we?" asked Bear.

"Truly?" said Frog.

"Are you sure?" said Snake.

"We're sure!" said Leopard and Woodrat. "There aren't any rules about being friends, you know. See you tomorrow!"

"See you tomorrow!" said Bear and Frog and Snake.

*"I can bound and bounce," says Little Ghost.*

*Big Ghost nods. "I'm sure you can."*

*"I'm going to bound and bounce all the way home," says Little Ghost, and off he goes.*

# WEEK 51

*Big Ghost is sitting on the roof when Little Ghost arrives.*

*"Hello, Little Ghost!" he says. "Come and sit down. There's a wonderful view from here! We can see just what the weathercock sees ... "*

## North, South, East, West

We look to the north, and what do we see? A line of trees, and a road and a –.

Whoops! The wind's blowing!

Round and round and round and round and round we go.

Until we stop.

We look to the west, and what do we see? A garden of flowers. Roses, marigolds, daisies, and vegetables too. Crisp green cabbages, luscious lettuces, shiny red tomatoes, rows of little radishes and ...

Whoops! Here's the wind again!

Round and round and round and round and round we go.

Until we stop.

We look to the east, and what do we see? A field full of long grass, with thistles and yellow flowering gorse. We can see a stream rippling and sparkling, and hedges of holly and elderberry, beech and thorn.

Whoops! The wind is whistling …

Round and round and round and round and round we go.

We look to the south, and what do we see?

A green grassy lawn edged with flowers, trees, a path.

We see a man and a woman walking slowly, and a man and a woman arm in arm.

We can see a tall boy, a small boy, twins on a swing, and a very little girl picking daisies for a chain …

We see dogs bouncing after a ball, a cat on a step and a cat on a tree.

A cat asleep on a wall …

And a kitten chasing a big pink butterfly.

"I know who those people were!" says Little Ghost. "It was Granny Annie and Jason and Daisy B and the twins and Ross, wasn't it? And Mum and Julius and Visiting Dad. And Hunter and Tiny and Fat Freda and Big Tom and Kitty Purr! See? I remember all their names!" And then Little Ghost sighs and looks sad. "Except the kitten. I do so wish I knew his name."

"Come with me," says Big Ghost, "and be VERY quiet."

Little Ghost follows Big Ghost down and down through a window, and there is Daisy B, fast asleep. The kitten with no name is curled up beside her, purring softly.

"Daisy B doesn't know what to call him," whispers Big Ghost. "Could you help?"

Little Ghost watches the kitten yawn, stretch and curl up again. He nods and tiptoes nearer the bed.

"Tiger!" whispers Little Ghost. "Daisy B, call him Tiger!"

Daisy B stirs a little, and puts out her hand. The kitten purrs louder.

"Hello, pretty kitty," says Daisy B, even though her eyes are tight shut. "Hello, my Tiger," and then she snuggles back into sleep.

"She knows his name! That's the name I chose!" Little Ghost is quivering with excitement.

"Sh! Time to go," breathes Big Ghost, and he and Little Ghost slip silently away.

He's called Tiger. What a nice name.

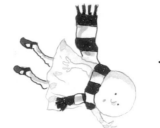

# WEEK 52

*Little Ghost has come in through the keyhole. Big Ghost is drooping by the stairs.*

*"Hello," says Little Ghost. "What's the matter?"*

*Big Ghost sits down on the bottom step. "Little Ghost," he says, "I've something to tell you."*

*Little Ghost sits down beside him. "What is it?"*

*"I'll tell you your story, and then you'll see," says Big Ghost.*

## The Last Story of all

Once upon a time there was a Little Ghost who loved stories. Once a week his mother went out haunting, and while she was busy Little Ghost would go and visit a big ghost who lived in an old house with a garden full of flowers and vegetables. The big ghost was old, and sometimes he was very sleepy, but Little Ghost would always wake him up and say, "Tell me a story!"

So Big Ghost would think of a story about the people or the animals who lived in the house, or sometimes it was a story about the children's toys, or the slugs and snails in the garden … and he had fun, and so did Little Ghost.

One day, however, Big Ghost ran out of stories. Little Ghost came happily slipping through the keyhole, just as usual, but he found Big Ghost in the hallway looking very sad.

"I'm sorry, Little Ghost," he said. "I don't know any more stories."

*Big Ghost stops.*

*"Go on," says Little Ghost. "Go on with the story." Big Ghost shakes his head. "There isn't any more, Little Ghost."*

*"OH!" Little Ghost's eyes are very wide. "You really truly don't know any more stories?"*

*Big Ghost nods. "That's right, Little Ghost. I've told you evey single story I know."*

*Little Ghost thinks for a moment. Then he smiles a huge smile.*

*"I know," he says. "It's easy! You can tell me your stories all over again!"*

*Big Ghost looks surprised. "Are you sure?"*

"Oh YES," says Little Ghost, and he settles himself down. "Stories are even better the second time around"

There's a scratching on the front door. Little Ghost and Big Ghost look up, and see a very small ghost squeezing himself through the keyhole.

"Hello," he says. "I'm Baby Ghost. I've come to listen to the story."

Baby Ghost cuddles up with Little Ghost, and Tiger the kitten curls up beside them, purring loudly.

Little Ghost sighs a long happy sigh. "We're ready, Big Ghost," he says.

So Big Ghost begins at the very beginning:

Once upon a time there were four little kittens.

Bye, see you next time.

Which story did you like best?